Other titles in this series:

Her mission is about to get real. And *hot*...

Marine Tyler Knight wanted to make it home for the holidays. Truly, she did. But when her current mission in the Middle East goes awry, getting back in time for tree decorating and eggnog is the *least* of her concerns. Worse yet, she might have to do the unthinkable and accept help from her brothers' best friend and special ops teammate—a man who almost makes her forget she's a badass who doesn't *do* romance...

Bo Hawkeye loves strong women, but Tyler is *impossible*. The fact that she's also beautiful, sexy as hell, and awakens his every protective instinct *shouldn't* matter...but it does. So, he'll do whatever it takes to help her get home to her family—*and* convince her how good they could be together...

Can Tyler and Bo stay alive long enough to get to happily ever after? It might just take a Christmas miracle...

O Christmas Knight

by

Em Petrova

Chapter One

The finish line was in sight, and Tyler was damn well getting a personal best time today. Her thighs were already burning from her flat-out sprint uphill the last mile, but she had it in her. She was a Knight.

Her commanding officer stood waiting for her, a stopwatch in hand. "Move your ass, Knight!" she yelled, and that was all the push Tyler needed.

She hardly felt the road under her feet and ignored the sting of sweat in her eyes as she strode for the last few hundred yards of the drill. She ran it daily, and hell, after twenty-mile treks through woods and mud in full gear, running ten miles unhindered on a road made her feel as light as air.

The unseen clock was ticking in her ears, but she ran faster than the rhythm of that sound and crossed the finish line to her commanding officer shouting her time. "45:01!"

"Dammit," she rasped as she downshifted to a jog and circled the finish line several times.

"Tell me you're pissed at that time, Knight, and I'll say you're a tougher little shit than I ever believed." Her CO was a hard ass woman made of grit and nails cemented together with sarcastic comments. From day one she'd nicknamed Tyler "little shit" which sure beat her brothers calling her Tyleri, a more feminine play on her boyish name.

Tyler shot her CO a look. "Gebrselassie did it in 44:24 flat out on the road in The Netherlands."

Her CO never laughed, but her eyes crinkled at the corners. "You're seriously comparing yourself to another runner? I thought you were seeking a personal best, and you did it. Here, have a water." She reached down at her feet into a cooler and plucked up a bottle covered in ice water. She tossed it to Tyler, and she caught it with ease. Five big brothers had taught her to either catch—or dodge—whatever was coming her way. Smelly socks being one of the things most dodged in the Knight household.

She twisted off the cap and brought the water to her lips just as the next woman crossed the line, almost a full minute behind her. Okay, so maybe she *was* a little proud of her time.

"You've got another thirty seconds to recover, Knight, and then I want to see you hitting those ropes." Her CO nodded toward the wall. Twelve feet tall with several ropes thrown over.

Tyler dropped the bottle into the dirt. "I don't need thirty seconds." She took off and swore she heard a laugh behind her. But no, that couldn't be her CO. She probably hadn't even laughed in infancy when a rattle was shaken at her.

Tyler threw herself at the wall with all she had. Hand over hand, digging in the toes of her boots to propel her up and over. She dropped the distance in a freefall, landing in a crouch and then rolling as she'd been taught during some of her first days of basic training.

There stood another officer. "Good work, Knight."

"Thank you."

She filled her lungs with a big breath of air and launched to her feet, sprinting toward the next obstacle. This one a belly crawl through filth that would send her twin sister Lexi into shrieks. As sisters, they were as different as night and day, but Tyler often wondered how they'd shared the same womb. All she could figure was Lexi must have decorated her half with flowery pillows and room scents to make it through the ordeal.

She almost laughed at the vision of her very girly sister floating amidst all the feminine things she loved. Flowers in particular. It was no wonder she loved her job at the local flower shop.

Tyler flopped into the muck. And this wasn't just mud. It reeked of manure.

Breathing through her mouth against the stench, she dug in her knees and elbows, moving as fast as she could through the shit and... pig parts? Yes, the higher-ups had felt it a good idea to make them crawl through body parts with swarming flies. She passed by a hoof and turned her face aside. No way was she going to admit her stomach was turning. She was made of tougher stuff than that.

3

I'm a Knight.

If only her brothers could see her now. She'd heard enough of their self-praise at home and their legendary acts had followed her all through basic training, so the only way to get out from under the yoke of their prowess was to top them.

Which so far, she was. Her time had to be excellent.

She ducked under barbed wire but felt metal catch her shirt. She ripped it free with another thrust forward. Crap clung to her neck and soaked even her sports bra, and she couldn't wait for the next leg of this course, which was the plunge into the lake and a quick swim.

"Damn, Knight. I've never seen anyone crawl so fast through that." The next officer leaned against a jeep, legs crossed, staring at her rather than the stopwatch in her hand.

She'd grin but she'd risk getting shit in her mouth. So she pressed her lips shut and wiggled to the end, over a carcass with a final heave of pure determination.

Hauling herself to her feet after that took a bit more willpower than she was expecting—she felt suctioned into the muck. But she made it, lurching forward without pause. The water twenty yards away was a welcome sight. She could almost feel that cool water washing away the sweat and so much more on her body.

She felt like she could swim the Mississippi at this point. She was riding a high, had this in the bag. Guts and glory one mission at a time, was a motto of her brothers' Knight Ops team. Well, she definitely had the guts, and the glory was hers, right after this swim.

She dived in, dunking her head to wash the sweat out of her eyes and God knew what else. Her arms moved automatically, pistoning over and over, pulling herself easily through the water toward the other side.

With the repetitive action, she felt her mind wandering to the last time she'd been home, and how she'd missed her brother Chaz's wedding to a woman named Fleur. She'd seen photos of the pair, and Lexi had been in the wedding party, dressed in a blush-colored slip dress surrounded by flowers and looking lovely as usual. The bride and groom had been glowing with happiness, and Tyler had stared for a long time at them, feeling a pang of regret for missing it.

In some other pictures, she was able to piece together their entire reception. White cake towering high, a Conga line meandering through the chic hotel reception room. Each of her brothers showing signs of fatigue, probably having just returned from some mission but damn happy — and damn lucky — to have made it to Chaz's nuptials.

And in the background was extended family and many friends, including Rocko, the odd man out on the Knight Ops team, the only guy who couldn't boast Knight blood running through his veins. And Bo Hawkeye, aka Hawk .

Hawk was a weird individual, and one Tyler couldn't quite wrap her head around. He hung out with her brothers, was still very close to his ex-wife, who happened to be her brother Sean's new spouse.

Yeah, Hawk was a wild card. He fit with them, yet he didn't. He came and went like one of those Windwalkers of the Cheyenne Indians, almost a spiritual entity who flew in and out of their family but never touched down completely.

Tyler was ten feet from the shore, and she could finally say she was tired. She couldn't wait to drag herself onto that bank and lie there with her face lifted to the sun so it could dry the droplets from her skin. She shook off thoughts of home and any homesickness she'd let seep in even for a minute. Two more hard kicks and her knees struck the soil bottom.

She towed herself up onto the dirt and the officer standing there grinned down at her. "Well done, Knight. I'd say you've lived up to your family name."

About fucking time.

* * * * *

"Goddammit." Hawk felt the vein in his temple bulge as his blood pressure hit numbers he didn't want to contemplate. He sliced his hand through the air at Frisco. Two slashes of his hand meant go forward. Three to the left. He sent him forward, and Frisco rallied his three-man crew and followed orders. When they got to a ledge, their bellies hit the dirt and they switched to a crawl.

He didn't dare utter a whisper into his comms unit to tell them how to perform—he'd have to trust that his team was as badass as the terrifying bayou werewolf they were named after, Rougarou.

His other teammate, Corporon, hung by Hawk's side, awaiting orders, his face grim. Sometimes Operation Freedom Flag sent them into the most fucked up situations, all in the name of eradicating homeland terrorism. But the South was a hotbed of activity. And Louisiana provided enough ground cover to hide all the crazies, it seemed.

But Team Rougarou knew these swamps better than anybody. They were good old bayou boys, every one of them, born and raised knee deep in gator-land. They outwitted any idiot with firepower and an agenda who stepped foot in these swamps.

Right now, Team Rou was out-manned three to one. No matter. Hawk and his guys would neutralize the threat and come out alive.

Over the past year and a half the special force had been assembled, they'd only lost one teammate. McMahon had been a hell of a warrior, and Hawk had been honored to call him friend. He died with honor, the same as they all wanted to when it was their time.

But not today.

"Ease left," he breathed into his communication device, and the three on the ledge slithered sideways. He turned to look at Corporon and Depeux next to him. "They take the high ground and we go around. Go!"

Depeux scrambled to his feet like a man who wasn't laden with seventy-five pounds of gear, and Corporon followed with Hawk overtaking them to get in the lead. These assholes had been holed up in the swamp long enough. After evading New Orleans police, they'd been hiding in the swamps for days in a standoff that had finally gotten Team Rou called in.

Right off, Depeux had determined they knew jack shit about the explosives they were threatening to detonate—for love of country, as any political radical would say. They weren't just dangerous but stupid, which was an even more fatal combination. They had enough explosive to take out half of the bayou, but they only had it rigged to blow a small portion. Hawk was betting on their stupidity to see them captured.

"Close the noose," he ordered to his team, and they converged on the group's location. When shots whizzed by Hawk's ear, he realized they'd been spotted, but no matter.

The three he'd sent to the ledge opened fire, cutting off half of the group of men who were out to kill them. Hawk kept his three-man team down, at a better advantage since the radicals wouldn't know exactly where the bullets were coming from.

Swamp water swirled around his Gore-Tex military issue. Ripples reached him as another body hit the swamp with a sickening splash. What a terrible waste of bullets, he thought. The assholes should have just drunk poison Kool-Aid like so many other groups like this one who popped up in the South.

The Knight Ops team joked about Mississippi being a hotbed of activity for nut-cases, but Hawk would lay his money on good old Louisiana every time. The shit they saw here... there was a new cockroach king slithering into the swamps every damn day.

"Now!" Hawk's order rang out, and they jumped up, spraying bullets at anything that shot at them. The moment felt oddly like one of those carnival games played as a kid, where you shot a BB at metal ducks until you had enough tickets to win a teddy bear. Hawk was sure he still had one of those neon-colored bears with staring eyes somewhere in the attic of his parents' house.

Bodies dropped with splashes.

"Watch the gators, guys. They smell the blood." Frisco's warning brought Hawk out of his memories and he looked around himself.

"There are two more. I counted nineteen in all. Spread out, search the swamps. Watch your six," Hawk said.

They fanned out, ignoring any gators coming in to feed on the blood they scented. Swishing through the water with weapon at the ready, Hawk focused on the trees springing up out of the murky water. Good hiding places for anybody if they crouched low enough.

"Look to the trees," he ordered. "Keep sharp."

A shot rang out, and he turned to watch a body drop.

"Nice work," Wolf said to Frisco.

"Down to one. It's you and me, asshole. Show yourself," Hawk muttered to himself, though his team heard him.

The sun was sinking in the sky, sending shadows through the swamps, but he and his men could pick out a person in the dark. He saw a shadow shimmering on the water, a shadow that was not a tree trunk or branches from above.

He raised his weapon and took the shot.

A cheer went up from the guys. It was a grim victory, but this game was kill or be killed.

Hawk surveyed the waters. "What a fucking waste. Not one of them showed signs of giving themselves up or backing down. Frisco, call Jackson and tell him we need nineteen body bags and a recovery team," Hawk said. "Our work is done, Team Rou. Good job." The thrum of adrenaline hit his system as he walked out of the swamp, giving him a hard-on. After years of this, he came to expect it, but it was never easy when he calmed down and found himself alone with no lover to slake his lust on and celebrate the fact he was alive.

Maybe tonight he'd head into the Big Easy and find himself a pretty little thing to dry-hump his thigh on a dance floor. Then cup her ass and grind his cock against her, showing her that she should pick him to come home with, not that he had any trouble with the ladies.

How long had it been since he'd had a soft woman in his bed? Months, though he had no real reason for his abstinence other than searching for women bored him these days. But his erection told him to get the hell over it and find someone.

"A team's on their way, Hawk," Frisco said with a white grin in his mud-smeared face.

Hawk pounded him on the shoulder before turning to make his way out of the swamp.

Oh yeah, it was time to celebrate this win.

Chapter Two

Tyler called herself a confident woman. She was as comfortable in high heels as she was in combat boots. But that didn't mean she couldn't still be intimidated, and right now, she could bite off all her fingernails, if she had any long enough to bite.

Being brought in front of Major Abigail Bishop, one of the only females to ever hold this title, was one of Tyler's scariest and proudest moments.

Feeling like she might either puke or kick up her heels in a happy jig at any moment, she walked the long corridor leading to the major's office. When the private on duty gave her a sharp nod and pushed open the door for Tyler to enter, she returned the nod and stepped inside.

The space was no-nonsense, just like the major herself, with a big metal desk and hard-looking chairs. Not even a picture frame of family could be seen. It seemed Major Bishop had exited the womb and landed directly in this chair.

Tyler made a mental note to tell her brothers that first chance she got just to see their reactions. They'd probably laugh—but she couldn't.

She snapped to a rigid salute. The major eyed her and then said, "At ease, Knight. Take a seat."

Whoa. This was big. Tyler was being offered a seat?

She sank to the chair, her spine straight and hands in her lap so the major didn't see her white-knuckled grips on the arms.

"I have some news."

All of a sudden, Tyler's façade crumbled. Her heart began to pound.

It had finally happened — one of her brothers had lost his life serving his country.

She bowed her head, struggling with tears that were ready to overflow like hot lava. "Which one was it?" she managed to whisper.

The major was still for a minute. "Oh. You think you lost one of your brothers. I'm very sorry to have led you to believe that, but your brothers are all safe."

She jerked her head up but knew her expression of shock and grief hadn't yet been wiped off her face. "They are?"

Major Bishop's expression softened. "Yes, they're healthy and safe, Knight. Do you want to take a moment?" She waved at the room in dismissal, and Tyler got up from the chair and walked to the windows that overlooked the lush green lawn and some shrubbery. She pinched her nose hard to fight back the tears of relief that now threatened to spill out.

Dragging in deep breaths, she watched a bird hop from one branch of the shrub to another, its black watchful eye curious. Staring at the bird helped Tyler collect her emotions and stuff them back inside.

She returned to the desk and resumed her seat. "Thank you."

She gave a hard nod. "You've shown amazing physical prowess while here, Knight."

"Thank you, Major."

"And a new personal best that also breaks all records on this base. Congratulations."

Tyler found a trace of a smile. "I would have liked a better time."

The major tipped back her head and laughed, and for the first time Tyler saw her as a woman with sparkling eyes. A laugh like hers would slay men's hearts. Tyler wasn't the only woman doing a job that, until a few years ago, only men did, and she admired each and every one.

"I admire your spirit, Knight. When given praise, you admit you're disappointed in yourself. But I've brought you here to tell you that the Marine Corps is not disappointed in you."

"That's good to hear, Major."

"I won't beat around the bush—we have a team ready to deploy to Kandahar."

Her heart hit her chest wall and pounded heavily.

"There's a small uprising there that needs attention. And we've had our eye on you for some time, Knight. You don't only display extreme physical prowess but a very sharp mind as well, and we need both, as it turns out. I'm assigning you as Civil Affairs Specialist."

Tyler's mind skipped back and forth across the title. "Would you please explain my duties, Major?"

"Basically you will be rubbing elbows with the civilians and government officials in the area. Putting yourself in front of them to let them know we in the United States have their best interests and safety at heart. But we also need you to open your ears."

Her heart drummed faster. "Intelligence."

Major Bishop wasn't about to commit to that word. "Every Marine must listen to what is being said around them and interpret that to make decisions. This is one of those times, Knight. We know you're up to it."

She gave a nod. "I am." Pride rose up, a cloud so heady that she could hardly see straight. "I'll do the Corps proud, Major."

She stood. "Good, then you deploy with Team Omega in forty-five minutes. I have transport waiting for you at the airstrip."

So soon. Tyler stood too. "What about packing?"

"Your bag and all the gear you need is already on the aircraft." She braced her legs wide and eyed Tyler with—dare she think it?—admiration. "Good luck, Knight." He stood and dismissed her.

She saluted and turned for the door, hardly able to wrap her brain around what was happening. She was really getting her first mission, and for one so young and new to the ranks, it was an honor above anything she could have asked for. It crossed her mind that her big brothers had paved the way for her, laid down their reputation and she was just benefitting, like a little sister in high school who got preferential treatment from teachers because her brothers were well-loved.

But she couldn't think about that right now. She would prove herself, give her all.

Semper Fi.

The Marines' motto branded her, and she raised her jaw a notch.

She was directed to a jeep that drove her to the airstrip and then was ushered across the asphalt to the military aircraft. From there, she met her new team—all hard, callused and scarred men who eyed her with amusement, like they'd just wandered across a kitten in a war zone. She stiffened her spine and held her own. These guys couldn't intimidate her, not when she dealt with five chest-thumping, arrogant asshole brothers every day of her life.

* * * * *

The first time Tyler had ever been fired at, she'd rolled to safety and marveled at the sound the bullets made striking objects around her.

16

The second time bullets sprayed over her and her team, she got out her weapon and fired back.

As her brothers would say, shit had gone sideways, and it was a damn good she'd proved her ability in intelligence as well, because she'd barely returned to Team Omega to warn them before the first shot was fired.

She popped over the stonework wall and squeezed the trigger, her ears exploding with heavy fire coming from the men next to her.

Dammit, this wasn't supposed to happen. She'd spoken to the officials who'd promised peace, yet here they were trying to kill her and the five guys she'd come to know as brothers and love just as much during her last two weeks here.

"Woolworth, don't take your time! Get the launcher ready," her captain bellowed.

Out of the corner of her eye, she saw Woolworth, a huge man with green eyes, a tiger tattoo on his right upper arm and a ready grin lift the grenade launcher to his shoulder with practiced ease.

"Duck and cover your ears, Knight!" he called out.

She hit the deck and pressed her palms to her ears as he fired. The explosion made pieces of stone crumble off the wall and rain down on her. Confusion clogged the air, along with dust. So much fucking dust. This country was all dust and fear, from what she knew from her short time here, but she had never

17

expected that her team's overtures for peace and a settlement in the dispute would come with this heavy price.

A rich laugh rose from Woolworth, and Captain March gave another order to strike hard.

Each of her moves was reflexive after all the training she'd had, both with her father, then brothers, and finally the Marines. Before now, though, she'd been aiming at a paper target. Now she was shooting to kill for real.

There wasn't time to dwell on that, not when they were under siege, outnumbered and pinned down in a fucking house that could be easily flattened. Suddenly she realized if the Afghan government wanted her dead, there wasn't much she could do about it. Not with air strikes being so prevalent in this area.

She reloaded and unloaded — watching a man fall from her bullet for the first time. It wasn't a victorious feeling like playing a video game, yet she didn't have time for the nausea rising in her gut. She shoved it down and got angry.

"Well, look at the prom queen, opening up hell's fires on these guys," Woolworth drawled out, and everybody laughed but her. Was this what her brothers were like? Making jokes during missions and under heavy duress? She imagined Ben and Sean cracking jokes and the others laughing.

Two hours later, nobody was doing much laughing, though. Captain March was on the phone,

18

blasting orders at anybody who would listen. They needed backup and they damn well needed it immediately. They were sitting ducks in this house and they required assistance right the fuck now.

Someone placed a hand on her forearm, and Tyler looked down at it and then up into the face of her teammate Joe Paris. The guys called him Joey but she just called him by his last name. At first, he hadn't liked her, but as soon as she'd approached the Afghan official she was to meet with and spoken the Dari language with a pretty damn good accent, if she did say so herself, Paris had given her more respect.

"Take a break, lay low for a few minutes. You've been at it for hours, and there isn't a lot we can do right now," Paris said in his low voice.

She nodded and lowered her weapon, just now realizing her arms ached with fatigue. She leaned against the wall, feeling the stone pressing into her spine in the painful knots there, but taking comfort from its solidness that had acted as barrier between her and so many bullets.

In a crouch, he turned to go.

"Paris," she called him back.

He swung his head around.

"Why haven't they just leveled this place, especially after we fired the grenades?"

He grinned. "They're keeping us alive as a power play. Anything else?"

19

She started to shake her head and then thought of something. "Yeah. I wasn't the prom queen."

He chuckled. "That doesn't surprise me, Knight."

She watched him crouch-walk back to the house a few yards within the wall. At some point the wooden door had been blasted into shards, and she couldn't imagine what else was destroyed inside.

She rested where she sat, breathing hard and replaying her first kill in her mind's eye. Then she promptly cut off that movie reel and focused on more productive thoughts. Like the upcoming holiday season. Thanksgiving with her big family, bigger now that her brothers had all brought wives home. The table would be bursting, elbow to elbow with people. A big Cajun Thanksgiving prepared by *Maman* and Lexi. Her mother would wave off praise as usual but Lexi would soak up the compliments and pretend to be so exhausted after slaving over the meal all day.

She missed her twin. Missed her family. And she wanted to get home to them intact.

The first explosions trembled the ground beneath her, and she scrambled to her knees.

"We need that backup anytime, guys," Captain March said calmly into the phone and then dropped it in order to raise his weapon. "Naptime's over, you pansy asses! Grab your balls and your weapons and say a Hail Mary!"

He opened fire and Tyler did the same. During a break in the noise, she called out, "I don't have any balls, Captain!"

He laughed but was too focused on leading them to say more.

After two more hours of heavy fire, it was a wonder they had any artillery left, but of course they didn't come to Kandahar unprepared. They'd tried for peace and had instead gotten locked inside a house on the edge of town for hours on end. Just as they relaxed, thinking it all over with, the war began again. The long hours of night were the worst for Tyler. She lost morale half a dozen times at least but rediscovered it just laying deep inside her in a hidden well she didn't know she possessed.

By dawn, though, she was bleary-eyed and she'd lost count of the bodies she'd watched fall. She dropped her head back against the wall, and her helmet tipped forward to cover her eyes. "When is that backup coming, Captain?"

"Anytime now, Knight."

"Where the hell are they coming from— Antarctica?"

Several guys laughed but she knew they were thinking the same. She saw the intense burning in their eyes that must reflect her own. She couldn't remember what they were even fighting for anymore and wondered if they knew either.

Her shoulders relaxed from sheer exhaustion and she drifted for a few moments, her ears still ringing from the shattering noise she'd endured for hours on end.

When the next siege jerked her to alertness, fury struck. She got to her feet and lifted her weapon.

Then she started crawling over the wall to shoot the bastards attacking them at closer range.

* * * * *

"Jesus Christ!" Hawk saw the Marine mounting the wall, exposing himself, and his heart gave a hard stutter. Sneaking in from behind undetected had been no easy feat of tactics, but he'd been given the leadership role of the reconnaissance team for a reason.

He and the eleven men he was leading weren't leaving the area without these six on Omega.

"Knight!" The roar came from the team's captain.

Hawk almost came unhinged. Knight? Rumor was that all five brothers by that name were right now deep in the heart of Alabama dealing with some dirty shit. It couldn't be any Knight that he knew.

Yet when Hawk peered harder at the person determined to blow through the lines like some kind of goddamn GI Joe, he recognized the smaller figure of a female.

Goddammit, it's GI Jane.

22

Hawk moved before he even willed his muscles to. He zigzagged through the courtyard in front of the house through a hailstorm of bullets and reached the front wall just as March dragged Tyler Knight back down to safety.

She sat there for a moment, dazed as March blistered her ears with a telling off that would make a man's gonads shrivel. But Tyler simply took it with a nod, twisted to face front again and took aim.

The fighting went on for all of half an hour before the real backup came in the form of a blast that shook the house on its foundation but wiped out the enemy.

In the hell of battle, Hawk had lost eyes on Tyler, and he was almost afraid to look around at the casualties their teams had taken, if any. He knew two of his guys had experienced minor injuries and had continued to fight despite their pain.

One of the guys let out a low whistle. Then the typical burst of laughter traveled from one to another—pure relief to be alive given voice.

Hawk got to his feet and glass crunched under his boot. None of the windows had made it and it was a damn wonder there had been only two injured.

One of his teammates gave him a grin, teeth white against his brown skin. Sweat poured out from under his helmet.

Hawk raised his jaw in acknowledgment of a job well done and moved through the house and to the wall.

Slumped against the stone was a figure, smaller than the rest but still bulked out in gear. His heart gave a wild gallop, thinking her dead. Then she raised her head and let out a whoop of victory that had the rest of the men on her team cheering. One reached down and grabbed her by the hand, pulling her to her feet. He thumped her on the back, and Hawk was aware of how small she looked compared to the big Marine.

How the fuck had she even come to be here? He hadn't gotten wind that she'd been deployed. Of course, he hadn't spoken to any Knights, not even his ex-wife Elise, in weeks. He'd come straight out of the swamps with nineteen body bags loaded into a truck and gotten news from the Pentagon that there was a situation and his skills were needed outside of the Homeland Security division OFFSUS, Operation Freedom Flag Southern US.

Another guy swept Tyler up in an embrace, and she pounded him on the back.

For years, Hawk had viewed her as the little sister, someone to protect. He narrowed his eyes, watching for some telltale interaction that revealed more than simple team camaraderie. No one was going to fuck with the Knights' sister.

The Marine let her go, and Tyler didn't look at him again.

With the fight finished, Hawk's guys came forward to grip hands with Omega. Hawk was aware of Tyler's position every second that ticked by, but she didn't glance his way. Had she seen him?

He broke away from Captain March long enough to circle the group, getting within ten feet of her. For a moment, he just examined her. A few cuts and bumps was all he saw, and she didn't appear to have any other injuries. He felt relief trickle through him, pooling in his gut. At least he wouldn't be facing the Knights with accusations that he'd failed to protect their little sister.

At that moment, she looked up, straight at him.

Their gazes locked and then they both twisted away. He couldn't acknowledge that he knew the other side of Tyler Knight, the girl who paraded around in a bikini on the dock of her family's bayou cabin. That woman wouldn't want her fellow Marines to know such details, and Hawk was too afraid that looking at her would somehow show it on his face.

But why had she turned away from him? She didn't want to reveal her link to him either, which was damned odd. And if he was honest, fucking annoying.

The big transport trucks rolled up and they were all told they would be taken to Kandahar Air Base. At that point, he was separated from Tyler as she climbed into the other vehicle.

With her well-being out of his hands, he ordered his men to load up too and the entire bumpy ride back to the air base left Hawk brooding over that split second when he and Tyler had locked gazes. In that moment, he swore he'd seen relief mingled with fear there. But the threat was over at that point, so what was it she was afraid of? Surely not him.

An hour later he'd showered and changed into a fresh set of clothes and when he entered a mess hall to the sight of enough food to feed an army ten times the size of this group, he immediately sought out the dark brown hair of the woman he wanted most to speak to.

He strode right up to her. She stood there sipping a bottle of water like she had no clue who he was.

"Tyler." He bit off her name through his clenched jaw.

She looked up but didn't quite meet his eyes.

He locked a hand on her arm and spun her to face him. "What the hell is your problem?" he whispered furiously.

She jerked her arm free and walked out of the mess hall. He followed on her heels, dragging her back around to face him. Her eyes, dark and full of sparks of anger, pierced into him. "We didn't need rescued."

He blinked. "You've gotta be fucking kidding me. You were pinned down for hours with no hope of putting an end to that attack. Your fucking captain called for backup!"

"You guys weren't there. You didn't face what we faced, and then you swooped in and claimed all the

26

pats on the back, you and your drone team that dropped the bomb on them!"

He ground his teeth. "Are you just pissed off that you didn't get to end it alone, six lone guys versus how-the-fuck-ever-many, all armed with assault rifles? Or are you pissed that it was my team doing the rescuing?"

She dropped her gaze and he ducked his head to force her to look at him.

"This was no time for heroics, Tyler. We already saw you nail at least five of those men in the thick of it. And I fucking saw you rush the wall like you were some invincible robot. What the hell were you thinking?"

She stared up at him. "What do you want from me, Hawk? You want praise? Are you looking for me to get on my knees and thank you for helping us?"

"Hell no. I just want you to acknowledge that we know each other on some level that is not this." He waved a hand at the landscape, so different from their home of Louisiana. Grayish sands and colorless buildings clinging to a corner of the world that in his opinion, wasn't fit for her to be in.

"Fine." She threw him a little wave and false smile. "Hi, Hawk. How are you doing? Would you care to grab some food from the buffet?" Her saccharine-sweet tone of voice grated on his nerves more than her avoidance.

27

He grabbed her by the arm again and dragged her several feet away from the door, out of earshot of anybody who might overhear their conversation.

"Let me go," she practically growled.

He released her but got up in her face. "Look, Tyleri—"

She winced at his use of the nickname her brothers had saddled her with. "Don't do that!"

He went on, "I *know* you're a badass. We all do. I've seen you do more pullups than me. But I've also seen your legs in a skirt."

He dropped his gaze to her lower regions and when he looked up, she was glaring.

"I know you're strong and tough as all Knights are. And what you experienced back there... what you saw... is enough to give SEALS fucking nightmares. Are you telling me you're above that?"

Right before his eyes, her façade crumbled. Her features screwed up like a baby's and she plastered her hand to her face.

"Jesus Christ, Tyler." He caught her against his chest, aware of how stiff she held herself and even beneath that, he felt her softness, the feminine side he knew and admired.

A soft sob racked her, and he gripped her tighter, a hand on her nape so she couldn't lift her head and show anybody but him that she was breaking down.

"Let's get out of here." He caught her elbow and led her quickly to the building he was housed in. By the time they reached the solitude of the space, her eyes were dry. But he could still see the effects of the past day on her. This was her first battle, and he remembered well how he had felt after his first.

She walked over to his bunk that he hadn't yet touched, despite the fatigue that weighed on him, and sank to it. He stood several feet away, watching her.

What would his friends, the Knight boys, have him do?

They'd want him to take care of their little sister.

"Why don't you lie down?" he said quietly.

She tipped onto the bed with a zombie-like movement that told him she was in shock. Jesus, maybe she wasn't cut out for this life at all. Then again, he'd seen grown men do the same thing following the fierce stress of battle.

She curled onto her side and closed her eyes.

He could stand it no more. He moved forward and climbed onto the bunk next to her. It was far too narrow for his broad shoulders let alone both of them, but he made it work. Banding an arm around her back, he drew her against him.

For a long time, she lay there, hardly breathing. He watched her features carefully for signs of further distress. Too late to pull it back, he raised his hand to her temple and smoothed her hair. Then in an act of extreme stupidity, he leaned in and brushed a kiss across her forehead.

She didn't move.

"Can I get you something to eat?" he asked softly.

She shook her head.

Hell, she was so soft and near, and his body was stirring at the feel of her. All womanly curves wrapped up in camo, showing her vulnerability only to him. That was the worst threat to his libido possible. Because Hawk was first and foremost a protector, and she was rousing all the right — or rather wrong — feelings in him.

Before he could stop himself, he rested his forehead against hers. She dragged in a deep, shaky breath.

Their lips were inches away and if he didn't stop now, he'd never be able to explain his actions.

He started to get up, but she grabbed him, twisting a handful of his shirt front in her small but capable fist. That hand had killed in the heat of battle and now it was slaying his self-control.

"Don't go yet," she whispered.

"Okay." He ran a hand over her spine, feeling her relax by degrees even as his body grew more taut. She fit into the spaces of his body with perfect ease, all curves and sweetness.

He was fucking dying.

At least that was what he thought until she pressed so close that he couldn't measure the gap between their hips.

He stopped breathing, his dick hardening at an alarming rate and need raking over him. His first thought was fuck, the Knight boys were gonna kill him. His second was how long could he endure this sweet torture?

Give him the waterboarding instead.

Hell, losing all his fingernails would be better right now.

He looped an arm around her middle, prepared to hold her still if she started wiggling.

Suddenly, she let out a faint noise, almost a gasp. Up close, her eyes were full of the one thing he never, ever expected to find in the middle of an air base a million miles from home.

Desire.

* * * * *

"Fucking hell, Tyler. What are you doing to me?" Hawk breathed out a hard puff of air as if he'd just been shot in the stomach. Somehow, his reaction to her and the emotions coursing through her body all tangled up into one knot that could only be unwound with a hard, fast fuck.

She cradled his jaw in one hand. Then he slammed his mouth across hers at the same moment she surged upward. The clash was bruising, wild. He split her lips with his hot tongue, sweeping it over hers with a franticness that sent her pulse racing.

She tore at his shirt and he gripped each side of her standard cammie blouse. In one hard yank, he ripped the buttons right off the cloth. The top opened

31

to his exploring hands, but he had to push up the T-shirt she wore beneath. He ran his callused fingers over the crest of her breasts held in a black sports bra and then down to her ribs, tickling over them with a gentleness she never thought possible from a man like Hawk.

He wedged a knee between her thighs and rolled on top of her. The bunk creaked in protest of their combined weight, but she ignored the sound and focused on the harsh breaths he was struggling to take. Or maybe that was her. She didn't care—just get her clothes off and give her what she needed.

She tore his shirt overhead, giving her access to the hardest muscles she'd ever been privileged to touch. Her brothers were built, sure, but she only hugged them or punched them accordingly. This man... God, he was beautiful.

She dug her blunt nails into his shoulders, yanking him down on her. He angled his head and kissed her breathless even as he rocked his knee up into her pussy.

She moaned, and he let out a growl that rumbled through her entire body. Passion mounted, and she couldn't wait another second. "Take me," she breathed.

"Fucking hell," he said a second time.

He went for her boot laces first, reaching back and expertly untying them like he stripped Marines every day of his life. For all she knew, he did. Elise said Hawk had plenty of lovers, though Tyler had never seen him with anyone.

"I'm warning you I have no condoms and I'm not going to use them on you anyway." His eyes were dark, glittering with a challenge.

Which she stepped up and accepted. "I'm on birth control and I know you're as clean as I am."

"It's not just that. It's..." He struggled for a second and then gave a rough shake of his head. He never completed the sentence, but she didn't care because he managed to get her boots loosened enough that she could kick them off. His own followed.

They stared into each other's eyes for a long heartbeat and then attacked the rest of their clothing.

He groaned as he found her cotton boy-shorts underwear and traced the line curving under her ass cheek with a fingertip. Liquid heat pooled in her groin, and her panties grew damper.

He thrust his tongue into her mouth, stealing all thought of anything but having that impressive length she felt digging into her thigh sliding into her body. God, his erection was just as big as the rest of him.

She cupped his bulge, and he ground out a noise that sounded like an animal on its prey. If that made her the prey, she didn't care. She just needed all of this. This touching, being made to feel real after that ordeal and to slake some primal lust she hadn't ever thought she'd be the one to experience. She'd heard about battle lust hitting but that was men, and men had big hormones.

Apparently, she did too.

Or maybe she only had them for this man.

When Hawk nudged her thighs apart with his knee and slid a hand into the front of her panties, she held her breath.

"Goddamn, you're soaking." His black eyes flashed.

"And you're as hard as stone. Don't hold back another second. Get inside me—now!" Her command didn't wipe the stern expression off his face or ease the two lines set between his dark brows.

He shoved her cargo pants and underwear down and off, leaning side to side atop her to allow her movement. When she was naked and his cock was freed, she immediately wrapped her thighs around his hips and pulled him down.

He went dead still as she curled her fingers around his cock. She pumped him once, gliding her thumb over the rounded head that was wet with precum.

Their gazes connected, and she guided his cock to her pussy.

They were crossing lines in ranks, with her many ticks below him. Yet he couldn't deny her.

"Forgive me," he said with a violent shove of his hips, joining them hard and fast.

She bucked upward, sucking him deeper yet.

His body shook, and her own answered with a constant tremor of lust. Her insides quaked and her hands trembled where they kneaded his spine, urging him closer.

"I always knew you were trouble." He slammed into her, neck cords straining.

She laughed softly but the noise was cut off on a gasp as he withdrew. Each inch of his solid, impressive length slipping through her wet walls had her pussy clenching. When he reached the tip, he looked into her eyes and slammed home again.

They shared a cry, and she caught his lip in her teeth. A growl raised from him, and after that, he took total control. Grabbing her hip to lift her in time to his plunges and slanting his tongue through her mouth until she couldn't remember a time when he wasn't doing this to her.

Fucking her.

Almost making love to her.

Jesus, what was she thinking?

She was thinking Hawk felt amazing and she wanted to get closer.

She tightened on his next thrust. He burrowed deep into her channel, and when she started to pulsate, on the brink of coming unglued, he dropped his forehead to hers.

The intimacy of the pose carried her over the ledge of restraint, and she came with a sharp rasp of bliss. He fed her a groan of his own. Rather than stiffening and pumping hard and fast as many men she'd slept with did when they came, Bo grew cuddly. Winding his arm under her and lifting her against his chest, his hips pumping with a slow rhythm as the first hot splash of his cum hit her insides.

The sensation was shocking. She'd never had a man like this before.

Then the warmth struck again, and to her even bigger surprise, the feeling sent her straight into a second orgasm.

She floated, eyes pinched shut on the mind-numbing bliss as Bo continued to ride it out with her. Long after her final shudders faded away, he rocked into her.

"I can't quit fucking you." He was still hard as hell and she was still needy.

She grabbed his ass and held him to her. While small aftershocks had her clenching and releasing around him, a rumble ran through his chest.

All of a sudden, her actions hit her.

She'd just fucked Bo Hawkeye, her brothers' good friend. A man who often spent time at the family cabin with them and yes, had seen her legs in a skirt or bathing suit many a time.

He pulled back to look at her, his biceps bulging. His skin was tanned from the sun, a tattoo of the mythical Cajun werewolf that prowled the bayou, Rougarou, snarling at her from his solid pec muscle.

She pushed against his chest, forcing him to roll off. As soon as she was free, she leaped off the bunk, reaching for her clothes.

"We can't ever talk about this," she said.

He was silent. She drew on her abandoned underwear but she was still wearing her sports bra. He hadn't even gone for her breasts.

What was wrong with her breasts? Maybe they were too small for his taste.

She shook off her insane thought and stuffed her arms in her sleeves. When she found all the buttons gone or hanging by threads, she left it and reached for her pants.

He just sat there on the bunk watching her, dark gaze following her every move. He hadn't responded to her statement either.

"That's not a request, Hawk. We can't talk about this. The family can't find out. And you have to promise never to tell Elise."

"Why the fuck would I tell Elise?"

"Because you're still close friends."

"Yeah, but I don't tell her or anybody else who I've been with. Jesus, Tyler, you must think I'm a real asshole."

She glanced at him, fighting to keep from looking directly into his eyes because she didn't trust herself. That whole womanly part of her wanted to lie with him and be cuddled against his chest, to have him stroke her hair and share some softer, less urgent kisses.

But that would be a really, really bad idea.

Disaster.

She wrapped the side of her top over the other and stuffed the tails into her pants. It was makeshift at best, and she prayed she didn't run into any officers on the way to her own quarters. Them finding her with her top shredded open and bite marks on her throat wouldn't gain her any military honors.

She shoved her foot into her boot and stomped to settle it. Then the other.

Hawk still didn't move, just sat there in all the glory of his nudeness, more carved than even she had imagined.

He jammed his fingers through his hair, which was longer than the men she'd served with here in Kandahar. Since he was special ops with OFFSUS, he had more freedoms with his personal appearance. She'd even seen some of his teammates sporting beards.

She averted her gaze from the stiff cock still bobbing in his lap.

He didn't speak or reach for her either. That was best — she couldn't get cozy with this man, and so far the regret hadn't set in.

Yet.

She was certain those feelings would come later when she was alone and had time to think. She'd realize she'd been weak and asked for something she shouldn't have.

He pushed out a breath through his nostrils. "You're seriously leaving things like this?"

She turned her face away. It was hard as hell to walk away from a man that had just given her two amazing orgasms in a row and whose seed was still trickling from her swollen folds.

Unable to think of any response, she bit into her lower lip and nodded. Then she bent and tied her boots with haste and practically ran out of his quarters.

Luckily, she didn't pass anybody on the way to her own bunk—they were all tied up in the mess hall, celebrating their recent victory. She should be with her team too, but she couldn't bring herself to go back even if she didn't look like she'd just been ravished.

Well-loved.

Thoroughly loved.

God, Bo was a fucking great lover.

Her insides coiled at the memories fresh in her mind, spurred on by his scent all over her.

She had to get a shower and fast. Washing away the musk of his body and their shared pleasure still wetting her inner thighs was the only way to forget what had just happened.

But long after a hot shower, she lay on her own bunk, thinking of the man who hadn't been afraid to touch her, to meet her demands stroke for stroke.

That regret she expected to feel never hit.

Chapter Three

"Where's Team Omega?" Hawk's question came out rougher than he'd like, and the guys he'd fought with eyed him.

Between jet lag and the Tyler thing, Hawk had slept all of a few hours, and he wasn't in a fuck-with-me mood. He'd already searched the mess hall and the perimeters of each building on this dry plot of earth for sight of the woman who was haunting his every waking and sleeping moment.

"Shipped out this morning. Should be Stateside this evening."

"Goddammit."

The guys stared at him, and he couldn't let on that he was losing his grip. Though it was coming close at this point.

"One of the guys left something behind. I'll track him down once I get home," he said to cover his ass.

Glaring at the ground, he strode to the buffet and dumped food on his tray without even bothering to look what it was. It could be pig slop, for all he knew or cared. He had to eat because his body required it but he was far from hungry.

At least not for food.

Tyler had shaken him.

No, rocked him, more like.

Dammit, Earthquake Tyler had struck with full force, leaving him on uneven ground with pits and chasms all around him and no idea how to proceed.

She wanted him to pretend he'd never laid a hand on her.

He felt a growl rising in his throat and the guy next to him shot him a look. Hawk cut off the noise and grabbed two bananas. He was fucking boiling with anger over Tyler's actions. First, walking out on him and demanding he not kiss and tell. As if he would. She couldn't even look at him full in the face, and that rankled more than anything.

And she hadn't come to say goodbye either.

That he might be able to forgive. Knowing how the military worked, she might've had five minutes to pack her gear and load up. But when he got back to Louisiana, he was damn well going to hunt her down and clear the air.

If he didn't, this... *encounter*... would be hanging over them forever, creating tension where there didn't need to be any. Her brothers would notice, and Elise would have Hawk by the balls and squeezing till he at least admitted something had gone down.

No, he had to handle this.

He slammed his tray down on the table and sank to the bench. He also had to handle his thoughts on the matter.

He wasn't about to pretend he hadn't experienced the hottest moment he'd ever had with Tyler.

Women came and went in his life. The only one who'd meant anything to him he'd married. Both he and Elise admitted that their marriage had been a mistake. They'd been great friends but lacked heavily in the passion department.

Hawk had a trail of ladies in his past, but hell, he couldn't remember half of their names. Never had he wanted to curl around one of them and protect them while simultaneously making them scream his name over and over, not like Tyler.

He pushed out a sigh and unpeeled a banana, biting off half in one big chomp. Damn her.

When she'd gripped his shirt and given him those wide eyes, what was he supposed to do?

Put a stop to it then and there.

Sure, like you could have. She's gorgeous. And every inch of her athletic body had you keyed up.

He shook off thoughts of that distracting black sports bra and those boy-short panties.

His ex-wife made amused remarks about him being a metrosexual—that he liked to dress nice and see women dressed beautifully too. For years he'd helped Elise with her wardrobe and his own boasted excellent taste. So he did some envisioning of certain women's closets, and Tyler's had always confused him.

She was so duplicitous—part sultry Southern gal with short dresses that showed off her toned legs and part tomboy. He'd sometimes seen her sporting running shorts and a Marines T-shirt one of her brothers had given her knotted at the waist.

So he hadn't known what to expect under her government-issue camo, but the black, sporty undergarments had turned him on more than any lacy garment could have.

Fuck, now his cock was getting hard again.

He polished off the banana along with the second one and then forked up what seemed to be hash with some kind of meat. Out here, who couldn't guess what animal it came from. Could be goat, for all he knew.

The rest of the morning was spent with his team in a room with the blinds closed against the deadly Afghan sun and orders taken. Clearly this shit storm wasn't finished and the military was asking him and his eleven men to remain in the area and handle it.

Any other time, he'd be glad of the distraction and the chance to get out of the fucking Louisiana swamps with the rednecks and their constant supply of C4, but not this time. He wanted to get home and find Tyler—there was far too much unsettled between them.

He pushed out a sigh. The words 'in too deep' didn't even cut it in his case.

When they were dismissed, Hawk walked outside onto an area shaded with a canvas awning and looked out over the land. Tyler was somewhere over the Atlantic. Was she thinking of their night together at all?

He scrubbed a hand over his face.

"You look like you could use a smoke." One of the guys shook a couple cigarettes from the pack but Hawk politely refused. He was too hung up on the woman.

Why now of all times? He'd known Tyler since she was in high school. Hell, after she'd split to join the Marines, leaving behind only a note and a selfie of her newly chopped off hair, she'd still never done much more than dial into his radar through her family.

Now she'd firmly planted herself right in the middle of the screen, a blip with swirls radiating out from her and overtaking his world, like one of those category 5 hurricanes on the radar, the ones that flatten your house.

He dropped to a nearby chair and tipped the legs back to rest his spine against the wall of the building. Around him, guys smoked and chatted about nothing in particular, but Hawk tuned them all out.

After graduating from basic, Tyler had spent over two years on base training new recruits with her physical skill set. In that time, he'd hardly seen her, and she'd both changed and hadn't.

Grown more athletic, leaner but with curves in all the right places. The hair she'd lopped off had grown back lush and thick. And last night with it tumbling around them…

Fuck. In too deep.

One sip of crystal-clear water from a spring of life had taken over his thoughts, and he wasn't even dehydrated. He didn't need to go looking to get laid. Pussy was pussy.

Unless it was Tyler's pussy.

In his mind's eye, he saw her drawn brows after he'd called her by that ridiculous nickname Tyleri. He couldn't see why it even riled her, but she sure was adorable when irritated.

God, when she'd splintered around him, pulsating hard and fast on his cock —

"Change of plans, Hawkeye. In the meeting room, now."

He dropped the chair to the ground and jumped to his feet, a salute in place before he'd straightened completely.

The colonel eyed him. "Round up your men."

"Yes, Colonel."

As he marched his team through the building to the meeting room, the only sound was the thump of their boots on the floor.

As soon as they were in the room with the door closed, the colonel turned to them. "It seems our friends have ended the dispute for us."

46

"Sir?" Hawk inquired.

"A political war broke out between two groups and it seems they've taken each other out. Most of the leaders are dead. Which means you're going home, boys. Transport in thirty minutes — be on it."

* * * * *

Tyler pushed out another long, useless sigh. Even though she'd lectured herself that she couldn't do anything about Team Omega's transport being grounded, her body longed to get in the air and homeward bound.

She'd had hours to think about holiday travelers who got stranded every year, miles from their love ones. That led to thoughts about her own family expecting her home soon, but that might not be possible now. She had no clue what was next in store for her.

She looked out over the barren land and tried to convince herself that the faster she got out of this country, the better. Despite what she'd just lived through, that wasn't even the truth.

She was running from Hawk.

Bo.

The names intertwined in her mind and lifted an odd shaky feeling in her chest that she didn't like and had never experienced before. Yeah, she needed to get away from this place quickly so she could regroup in time to see him at the next family gathering her brothers and Elise dragged him to.

But she was stuck on this damn airstrip until orders came through to fly for home.

Someone tapped her on the shoulder, bringing her out of her deep thoughts. She looked into Paris's eyes.

"C'mon. Time to go."

"Finally?" she asked.

"Yup. There was some airstrike and civil war between political groups that kept us on the ground in the event they needed our aid. It's handled, so we're set to board."

The military aircraft had been sitting on the strip for hours, and she'd been staring at it so long that the shape felt familiar when she finally stepped onto the craft. She settled into a seat and Paris took the one beside her. The other guys of Team Omega spread out throughout the cabin.

She was finally off.

More minutes ticked by. The vibration of the engine gave her a funny reminder of body parts she had no business thinking of right now. She pushed the memories of Hawk to the back of her mind, under a thick layer of mental dust and caged by a fortress of steel no man could ever pick his way through to gain information. What happened between them would remain there, never spoken of again.

More men entered the hatch door, sporting gear and grins. "Hey, good to see ya again," one said to Captain March. They clasped hands.

Her heart stilled. No, it had stopped altogether.

This was the team that had come to their assistance yesterday.

Which meant Hawk would be ducking under that doorway any—

Fuck.

She turned her head aside, a feeling in her stomach that wasn't *all* dread. She wasn't examining what the other portion really was and why it gave her a weird tingly sensation.

Heavy boot steps paused next to Paris. A big hand reached out and tapped Paris's shoulder.

"You're in my seat," Hawk said.

Paris looked around him. "Don't see your name on it." He wiggled his muscled form, settling more firmly in the seat Hawk was demanding.

"And I've got seniority on you, asshole. Beat it."

Paris remained unmoving for a long second, and Tyler glanced up to see the men having a stare-off.

Finally, Paris stood and moved to a seat farther back the craft.

Before Hawk's ass hit the seat, Tyler shot out, "You're a rude motherfucker, you know that?"

"Yeah, and you've still got the mouth of a trucker."

"Or a Marine."

"Touché." He stuffed his bag between his boots and looked at her, brow raised.

Damn him for looking so damn gorgeous. Why did her body have to react to him this way? She dropped a glance to his hands, feeling once again the callused, thick fingers moving over her slick, tormented flesh.

She looked away.

"You left pretty quickly yesterday."

"Hawk." Her tone brooked no talk about it.

"I could use my seniority over you and order you to talk."

She glared at him until the corner of his mouth tipped up in that devilish smile that won many a woman's hearts from what she'd heard.

"All right, I can't force you to talk to me. But I can sit next to you for the next sixteen hours and bug the shit out of you."

She turned her head away from him. "I have no doubts you will, too."

He chuckled, a low, deep rumble that she felt far more sharply than the jet's vibrations.

A few minutes later, they took off, ascending quickly. Tyler used the time to quiet her mind and focus on anything but the man at her side.

"Have you heard from your brothers lately?" he asked.

She glanced his way. "Not for a month or so. I had them all on a Skype call just before Chaz got married."

"Ah yes. Nice affair. Sorry you missed it."

"Me too."

"Lexi looked lovely in a spring green dress," Hawk said.

Amusement struck her. "You and your love for women's clothing."

He held up a finger, black eyes twinkling, damn him. "Not a love for women's clothing—a love for women dressed nicely."

"Got it." She wished she had something to do on this trip besides talk to her seat partner. It was like one of those horror stories of being stuck next to the chatty passenger on a domestic flight. Or someone who smelled.

If Bo smelled bad, it would be a lot easier to ignore the man, but the fresh scent of soap wafted off him.

She balled her hands in her lap.

He reached over the seat arm and stroked her knuckle, making her jump. She yanked her hand away but he drew back too.

Good, she thought even as her body warred with her.

It was time to lay things out there in terms he could understand.

She pitched her voice to a low murmur. "Look, Hawk, what happened shouldn't have. I'm sorry it did."

"You're sorry you came apart in my arms — twice?"

Oh God, must he remind her?

"You know what I mean. We talked about this."

"No, we didn't talk. You told me what was going to happen, but that doesn't mean I have to agree."

"Why do you have to be so difficult?"

"Just stating facts, Tyleri."

She closed her eyes and leaned her head against the seat rest, too exhausted for further argument. After a minute of silence, she hoped he got the picture, but when she stole a peek at him, she found him staring at her. Studying her, almost.

Crap, she was never going to shake him, was she?

She pushed out a sigh. "Tell me about home."

He slid his gaze from her mouth to her eyes, but the depths of his stare lost none of the intensity. Her skin prickled with awareness.

"Home is home. Same old city, a party all the time. I was invited to the cabin a few weeks back with Lexi and Rocko."

An uneasy coldness slithered through Tyler. She narrowed her eyes at him. "You better not be fucking my sister!"

That raised a laugh from him. Not just a low chuckle others would ignore but a big, booming laugh that had all the guys looking their way.

"You really do have bad opinions of me. No, I am not fucking your sister."

"Shh!" She cast a look around his huge shoulder to the back of the plane, but nobody was paying attention to them now.

"You Knights are extremely suspicious people."

"What's that supposed to mean?" she snapped.

"It means," he reached over again and closed his fingers around her tight fist, looking deep into her eyes, "you believe everyone is out to screw you over."

"How do you think we've managed to stay alive?"

He laughed again, just as loudly as before. He also kept his firm grip on her hand. "Sometimes, sweetheart, you just have to put your faith in other people. Didn't you just learn that lesson back in Kandahar?"

Chapter Four

After a while, Tyler drifted off, her head angled toward him on the head rest so he was able to study her beautiful face.

Dammit, he really was in too deep. Watching her sleep was doing things to his insides he'd never considered, and he'd seen plenty of women passed out in his bed. He was man enough to admit this woman was different.

But why? Because he already knew her through his friendship and camaraderie with her brothers?

Frustration also made his jaw ache. He wanted to wake her up and ask her why she'd turned to him back in his bunk and asked him to take her. Was it an easing of fear following her first battle or something else?

He searched his memory for moments when their worlds had brushed each other's. A holiday, a barbecue, one of Mrs. Knight's famous low-boil dinners at the cabin. Of course he noticed Tyler—she was a striking woman and not only for her beauty but for her confidence. Not once had he noted an odd look from her, a batting of eyelashes or any other sign of attraction.

Since he was so attuned to females, he'd know.

He'd never gotten so much as a long look from her, let alone a deliberate brushing of a shirt sleeve when reaching for a dinnerplate.

No, she'd never done any of those things. Then again, she hadn't behaved at all like the women he'd bedded in his past.

Hell, she hadn't even behaved like herself.

He pushed out a frustrated sigh and she rolled her head to a more comfortable position on the headrest. He stared at her plump lips, parted in repose, and felt his cock starting to harden.

He quickly glanced away. This was gonna be one hell of a long flight.

After she slept away most of the journey, he began to grow concerned that she might be ill. She hadn't seemed fevered but maybe she'd acted out of sorts because she'd been coming down with something.

She drifted in and out of sleep for hours, waking long enough to sip water or nibble on an energy bar.

Finally, she opened her eyes and he found them clear and bright.

"Feel better?" he asked. Part of him wondered if she'd been faking sleep and then decided that couldn't be the case. She'd simply been drawing on her reserves for days and it had all finally caught up to her. He'd experienced it himself.

She nodded and uncapped her water. When she took a sip, she winced. "It's warm."

"That's because you've been sleeping for hours. I'll get you another." He got out of his seat, stretching in the aisle so he reached almost to the ceiling of the craft and taking up all of the aisle.

She raked her gaze over him and then looked away. With a crooked smile of knowing, he moved to the back to get her a water. He came back with that and a packaged sandwich that looked like it had come from a vending machine. When he plopped into the seat again and handed these to her, she took them with a quiet "Thanks."

"Probably tastes like shit, but I know you haven't eaten much."

Her gaze shot back to his as she unwrapped the sandwich. "How the hell would you know?"

"Because you're slimmer than you were months ago when I last saw you."

"That doesn't mean I haven't been eating." Her tone was all barbs and spears, both keeping him out of her perimeter.

"What does it mean?" he asked.

"I've been training hard."

"Oh?" He settled back, sick and tired of sitting, but they had a couple hours left in the air. Then with luck, a good hotel bed and a tub big enough to hold him for a good soak. He almost groaned at the thought of hot water lapping around him.

She chomped down on the sandwich and tore a bit off ferociously. As she chewed, she said, "Been trying for a personal best and broke the base's record on the long course."

He laughed but not at her proud moment. "You eat like a Knight."

She glared and continued to chew in a way that might turn off any other man but him. He knew she didn't normally eat this way. She was trying to turn him off and make herself just one of the guys.

Except that ship had long sailed. The moment she'd clutched his shirt and given him those big eyes, he'd only seen her as his lover.

Fuck, in too deep, he reminded himself.

She swallowed and went in for another bite. "My record got me noticed and put me here."

"I doubt it's the first time you've been noticed, Tyler. You're hard to miss."

"I'm talking about being a Marine, Hawk."

"Who said I wasn't?" He arched a brow and held her gaze for a long heartbeat.

When she tore hers free, he saw a small pursing of her lips that he ordinarily would have missed. But since having her in his arms, he'd become far more attuned to her than anybody he'd been with.

"Proud of you, Tyleri."

Before he could draw a full breath, she jerked out a hand and clamped her fingers around his balls. His sac compressed by her hard grip and the pressure on

57

his nuts grew harder until his eyes just about watered.

But he was made of tougher stuff than that.

"You really don't relish having children, do you?" She applied just enough pressure that the water did come to his eyes. A big grin stretched across her face.

He didn't want to tell her that while what she was doing did cause an unpleasant ache in a place most men didn't want fucked with, her warm fingers were actually arousing the hell out of him.

He spread his legs and let her see his cock growing stiffer behind his fly.

Her gaze flashed down and pink rushed into her cheeks. She released him with a grunt of disgust and pivoted in her seat away from him, though there wasn't much room to escape.

When he chuckled, she shot him a dirty look that only amused him further.

Her wrapper crinkled loudly as she crushed it in her fist and fixated on scarfing down the rest of her sandwich. She drank off her water too and then stood.

"I'd like to go to the restroom." She was locked in by his legs, hers inches from his thigh.

For a split second, he considered tearing her off her feet and settling her over his still-hard cock. Of pressing his fingers into the spot that would make her moan.

"Hawk." She gave him the warning tone she probably reserved for her trainees.

58

He chuckled and got up to allow her to pass. But she still had to skirt around him and he was so big that meant their bodies touched. She quickly hurried down the aisle.

After that, time seemed to whiz by and soon they were touching down on US soil. That hot bath was sounding more and more promising. But then Tyler announced that she'd been given a month's leave, was renting a car and driving straight home to Louisiana.

He stared at her. "You can't be serious."

"Why not? I'm well rested and there's no reason for me to stick around in whatever location they put us up in."

He felt his shoulders, knotted for days, slump. No hot bath in his future.

"I'm coming with you."

She was shaking her head before the words left his lips.

Irritation rose up. "Why the hell not?" he said louder than he wanted and drawing attention from several of the guys.

"I'm capable of getting myself home." She pressed the back of her wrist to her forehead like a belle of old times swooning. "I'm not a lady who needs her fainting couch." She straightened and dropped her hand, bending to heft her heavy pack over her shoulder.

She took two steps before he groaned and picked up his own. At this point he wasn't sure if spending hours in the car with her driving back to New Orleans would make him desire her more or make him look for the first opportunity to ditch her. Probably both.

When he caught up to her, she stopped in her tracks. "Hawk, I'm going alone. But thanks." She didn't sound remotely thankful.

"Too damn bad." He reached for his phone and dialed a rental car place to come and drop one off for them in fifteen minutes. "There," he said, pocketing the phone again, "it's all settled."

"Elise never told me you're such a controlling man."

"Probably because I'm not." He grinned, suddenly not as tired as he thought. Hell, he could drive for hours with this kind of banter between them.

As soon as the rental arrived and he climbed behind the wheel, Tyler threw him a dirty look and walked stiffly to the passenger's side. She didn't say a word, just got in. He tuned the radio to an opera station.

She gave him the side-eye but her lips were pressed shut.

Smiling, he drove. After a few miles, he turned up the music on a particularly drawn-out, yodeling note.

Tyler just looked at him.

"This is where it gets really good." He sat back in his seat and pretended to feel the music.

Still nothing from the woman at his side, and he didn't know why he was goading her so much.

He tossed her a look. "You know, I could use some fresh air. The A/C always dries out my sinuses."

She gave him an are-you-kidding look.

When he rolled down his window the entire way, her hair began to swirl around her face. She brushed it away like an annoying fly.

How far could he push her till she snapped? The silent treatment was killing him.

"Do you take lessons off my brothers?" she finally burst out.

Biting back a chuckle, he gave her an innocent glance. "What do you mean?"

"They're the most annoying men on the planet and you're rivaling them right now."

"Only rivaling? I'll have to try harder."

He reached for the controls and rolled her window down too.

"Fine!" She released her seatbelt and twisted in her seat, leaning her torso out the window as if to tuck and roll in the middle of the highway.

"Fine! Damn. You really prefer air conditioning, don't you?" He pressed a button and her window rolled up.

She buckled again, simultaneously reaching for the radio control. When she got it to a hard rock station, he grinned.

After a mile or so, he chanced a look her way. She was staring out the window. "It doesn't feel like the holidays. I didn't realize there were decorations up."

"Decorations?" He looked out at the town they passed through, decked in garlands and sparkle. "We live in a fucking snow globe with Santa at the helm beginning in September."

She chuckled, a low, throaty sound that caught on his senses and slipped into his groin. "Being on base has kept me sheltered from it. Seeing it now puts me in the spirit."

If there ever was a woman who had two sides to her, it was Tyler Knight. Problem was, you never knew what you'd get — the sweet woman who could be wooed by a blow-up snowman waving from the front of a shop or the hard-ass who'd tuck and roll just because she didn't like your choice in music.

"You know, my brother Sean believed in Santa till he was thirteen. My brothers had to finally tell him because he was being bullied at school over it. Kids would say Santa wasn't real and Sean would beat the shit out of them." She smiled with a faraway look.

Hawk laughed. "I can totally picture that. What did he do when your brothers told him?"

"Beat the shit outta them too." She laughed again.

"Thing I love most about holidays is good food. Those MREs don't cut it for me. The last prepared military food I opened was supposed to be tuna and vegetables but looked more like something out of a Stephen King movie."

"Homecooked meals are always better. I could go for some of my *maman's* jambalaya. Or grits. God, her grits with all that butter..." She moaned in a way that had his cock thumping against his fly. Sudden thoughts of her laying her head in his lap and taking him in her sweet, hot mouth —

He was going to veer off the road if he didn't control his mind better.

They rolled out of the town and hit open highway again.

"Why aren't you taking the interstate?" she asked. "We just passed the sign."

"I like seeing America this way. Reminds me what I fight for." He threw her a look and found her staring at him like he'd grown a second head. He didn't want to tell her the one in his pants was swelling at an alarming rate.

"How did you get roped into coming to Kandahar?" she asked.

He pushed out a breath. "Guess they like my tactical skill. I literally came out of the swamps and was taken directly to Afghanistan."

"Why, when there were already units there?"

"I guess they wanted extra on standby."

"Do you get some time off now? Since you've been active on back-to-back missions?"

He snorted. "Honey, I'm practically operating for two different agencies. OFFSUS won't care if I've just come off a ten-day stint fighting in North Korea. If they need Team Rou on something, I'll be there."

She nodded, knowing full well her brothers also had experienced this with Knight Ops. The price of being one of the most elite teams was you were in high demand.

"Why wasn't your team with you? Rou?" she asked.

"They had the team I was with already formed. Just needed a leader."

She regarded him for a long minute. He could feel her gaze traveling over his profile and wondered what she was seeing there.

And if she liked it.

She'd like him buried deep in her pussy the other night, that was certain. He'd never known a woman to be so slick, so ready for him.

"You hungry?" He broke the silence before he drove off the road and hauled her across the seats into his arms. Her round ass planted where it belonged — in his lap.

She nodded. "I could eat something."

He ignored the leap in his gut at her agreement. He hadn't expected her to soften to anything he suggested, but her stubborn streak seemed to come and go like snowflakes on the wind, not that he'd seen many in the South.

Given some time, he could figure her out. If she let him.

When they hit the next town, rolling across a quaint bridge with arches spanning a narrow river, Tyler sat up straight and looked around. "This reminds me of a vacation my family went on when I was little."

"Yeah?" Damn, she was beautiful, more striking than ever with that sparkle in her eyes and a smile on her face.

"Road trips with all my siblings usually ended in disaster, but that was a good one. Hardly any fighting and my brothers took me and Lexi to get ice cream. I remember they bought us double scoops, and our parents never would have let us have that."

He met her stare, noticing not for the first time the green and gold flecks creating a sunburst around her pupils. "So you were getting your way even as a little kid."

"Getting my way? Ha. You can't imagine how hard it was growing up with five brothers who'd tried to get away with anything and everything, which only had our parents putting a stop to every stunt Lexi and I tried to pull."

"Which was why you took off and joined the Marines," he said slowly as it dawned on him.

"Yes. And why Lexi felt she had to sneak away to get some space to think a while back. She didn't tell you that when you came after her?"

He shook his head.

"That surprises me. I figured Lexi would have spilled her guts to you."

He arched a brow. "Why would you think that?"

"Well… you're easy to talk to, and Lexi is probably in need of a confidante now that I'm not around very much."

He heard the regret in her voice. "Do you feel you've let your twin down?"

Turning her face to the window, she said in a muffled voice, "We're close, so of course I feel that way."

"But you both need to march your own paths, Tyler. Lexi doesn't expect you to give up your dreams."

"I know that. I'm just being sappy because I'm on my way home. I'd actually get there too, if you'd drive faster than an eighty-two-year-old."

He stomped the gas, pinning her back in her seat.

* * * * *

Driving home to Louisiana with Hawk was one hell of a roller coaster. She had highs of liking him—a little too much—followed by spans of time spent wanting to kick him in the balls.

Halfway into Tennessee, he insisted on listening to the opera station again and she wasn't sure if he was just trying to tick her off or if he really liked it. When asked, he shrugged and said, "It's growing on me."

The man was completely insane and too damn hot for his own good. If they stopped for gas, females would hang out of car windows with their tongues lolling out like Labrador Retrievers. No wonder. If Tyler thought of Hawk objectively, she was well aware of his sex appeal. He looked like an action movie star who did all his own stunts.

Eating with him surprised her too. Not only did he not gulp down his food like a wild animal, the way most Marines did, but he used a knife and fork for everything besides the big juicy burger the previous night.

The thing was, she didn't mind sitting with him across a table because their conversation was always interesting.

He glanced over her shoulder and took a sip of his iced tea, foregoing the straw and drinking straight from the tall mug.

"What are you looking at?" Tyler asked.

"Two o'clock."

"Your two or my two?"

He gave her an exasperated look that almost made her giggle. "From your training, you know damn well it's my two. But don't look."

"What am I not looking at?"

"A woman. She keeps glancing over here."

Tyler didn't want to think of why her stomach knotted at that. By now, she knew every woman who came within sight of Hawk stared and sometimes drooled.

Tyler twisted her head and got a good eyeful of too much skin and cleavage from neck to navel.

When she turned to Hawk again, he closed his eyes with a shake of his head. "Good thing you aren't a spy, Tyleri. Your art of subtlety is severely lacking."

She threw the unused straw at him and it bounced off his muscular pec. "If you didn't want me to look, you shouldn't have drawn my attention to it."

"If I told you not to put your boot down because you were hovering over a mine, would you do that too?"

Ignoring his ridiculous comment, she said, "No wonder you were looking. There's a lot of flesh."

"That isn't why I was looking."

"Oh, you're saying you've been really doing a mental makeover of her?" She rolled her eyes.

"Yeah, I was."

She almost choked on her drink. "Seriously?"

"Yeah."

"You're an odd man, Robert Hawkeye."

His eyes flashed, sending a trickle of heat through her stomach. "That's the first time you've ever used my name."

She dropped her gaze to the worn laminate diner table and fought a flush that threatened to pop out in her cheeks. She'd called him Bo many times in her mind while he'd claimed her body. And countless times in her dreams since. Actually, she'd woken on the way from Kandahar several times with visions of him making love to her fresh in her mind. Instead of facing what she'd done with Bo, she'd closed her eyes tight until she drifted off again.

He ducked his head, catching her gaze and holding it. Unrelenting, unreleasing. A shudder tried to roll over her, but she steeled herself. The man wasn't making demands on her body.

She wrapped her lips around her straw and then lifted it from her tea and blew air fast. Tea sprayed across the table and wet the back of his hand.

His only reaction was to raise a dark brow.

Shivers worked deep in her stomach and dropped between her thighs. She clamped them shut on the sensation, locking it out. She was not attracted as hell to Hawk. She'd merely given into her need for a soft touch after what she'd endured back in Kandahar. It had been one moment of weakness, so why did her body insist on begging for more?

He slowly picked up his napkin, drawing her attention to his long fingers that had felt so good... so right all over her body... and wiped the tea from the back of his hand.

She pushed out a breath. "So what kind of makeover would you give her? Blonde hair, pushup bra?"

"You know me better than to believe I'm all about stereotypical sex appeal."

"So what would you do?" she pressed, actually wanting to hear now.

"Well, besides putting an actual blouse on her instead of that Band-Aid of a top, she needs short hair."

"Okay, why?"

"Her features are delicate and all that long stringy shit's weighing her down."

Tyler laughed out loud, a sound that rose up from her core. The man was fun to talk to even if he did drive her abso-fucking-lutely nuts.

"And what are you thinking? Ralph Lauren loungewear and boat shoes?"

He pushed out a sound, scoffing her off. "Again, stereotyping. She's clearly well-blessed in the top half, so she needs clothing to accentuate but not attract the wrong sort of interest."

Tyler cocked her head, examining him. "You're a crazy fucker, you know that, Hawk?"

He drank more tea and set down the glass. "I've heard it all before. If not from Elise then your

70

brothers. Just because I love to look at how women dress doesn't make me a perv or flamboyant."

"How would you make me over then?"

He stared at her for so long that she started to shift on the seat. And no, it was not because he was raising an ache in her pussy.

The waitress arrived with two platters of food — the hearty man's breakfast for him and pancakes and sausage links for her. She realized this would be the last breakfast they shared together. They'd been on the road for hours, and Hawk had refused to let her drive even once, which only revealed how much of a control freak he actually was.

The waitress paused at Hawk's side to smile at him for a heartbeat too long until Tyler said, "Thank you, that's all for now."

When she moved away, Hawk looked into her eyes, his face solemn.

"What?"

"You asked what I'd change about you."

"And?" Suddenly, she didn't want to hear what he had to say.

"Nothing," he said. "I wouldn't change a thing about you, Tyler."

Chapter Five

When they reached the rental car, Hawk held out the keys to Tyler.

She blinked. "You're letting me drive?"

The smile he gave her was a heartstopper. The corners of his lips turning up gently and his stare direct. "I'm tired. You know the way."

She snatched up the keys. "That means I get control over the windows and radio."

There was a spring in his step as he made his way to the passenger's side. She climbed in and he moved the seat back the entire way before sinking into it. Long legs stretched out, he reclined the seat as well, but his head still nearly brushed the ceiling of the small vehicle. It was impossible not to notice his size or remember how his big body had made her feel.

Protected. Safe. On fire.

She started the car and hadn't gone a mile before Hawk was asleep. Probably passed out from the arteries he'd just clogged with all that fat and butter, she mused. But the man was the picture of fitness and health. He could be a poster boy for any gym in the world.

She was feeling the effects of too much sitting and too much food during this trip home. The first thing she'd do was kiss her *maman* and then take a hot shower. She needed some sleep, but after that, she was going to run. The need to stretch her legs came along with a burning desire to take her mind off her companion. She'd spent too much time dwelling on Hawk.

Shooting a glance his way, she found his face turned her direction. The set of his features drew her in and she had to force her attention back to the road. He was gorgeous—why hadn't she ever really acknowledged it before?

It's just hormones. You slept with him. Of course your body is demanding more.

She turned on the radio, keeping it low so as not to wake him, and drove. She could have easily hopped onto the interstate and made better time, but thanks to Hawk, she looked forward to seeing what was in the next town. Small shops and people on sidewalks, probably discussing holiday plans. With a few weeks until Christmas, she imagined her *maman* already had their menu planned and gifts wrapped.

She rolled past a place selling fresh cut trees and could nearly smell the pine. What did Hawk do for Christmas? He had a sister and parents someplace, but would he go visit them? Or did he find some beautiful woman to hole up with for the day, wrapped in matching sweaters and cozy socks?

Tyler closed out that thought.

One thought led to the next and somehow she returned to what happened to her after the holidays. Back to the base and training more new recruits? Forcing them to achieve faster times that would in turn help them win wars?

The sounds of gunfire still echoed in her ears if she let down her guard. And that scared her. Since being pinned down in that battle, she was afraid she was damaged. Sure, she hadn't taken a bullet but the fear she still felt. The clamminess all over her body was real.

She turned on the cool air so it blew from the vents straight onto her face. She knew the signs of PTSD, had seen it on her brothers from time to time, though they always shoved it down and didn't speak of it. Now she wondered if she should have asked them about what they faced on their missions.

Town followed town and before long she was breaching the New Orleans city limits. The familiar sight of places she loved gave her an excited feeling. Soon she'd see Lexi and her parents, maybe her brothers and sisters-in-law and her little niece and nephew.

She missed so much of their day-to-day lives. Right now, she was glad to be home.

As she navigated the streets, Hawk awoke. He moved his chair into an upright position and looked out the window. He didn't speak for a long time. She'd never seen the man sleep, so she didn't know if he wasn't a person who talked the moment he opened his eyes or if he was dwelling on something too.

When they exited the city and entered the suburbs that stretched into bayou, she couldn't contain her happiness. The Spanish moss dripping off branches, the beauty of Louisiana, hit her hard and she choked up.

Of course, Hawk would guess the most inopportune time to speak to her and pounce on it. "Good to be home."

She only nodded.

"You all right?"

"Yes," she said with a gritty tone.

"You sound funny."

"Well, you look funny."

He barked out a laugh. "I guess my hope that when I woke up I'd find you sweeter has been crushed."

She pulled into her driveway and they bounced down the gravel lane leading to the big two-story home where she'd been raised. Only one car was parked out front, and it belonged to her mother. Her father would be at work and Lexi at the flower shop.

Tyler stopped the rental and put it in park. Hawk got out immediately and stretched. She averted her gaze from the rippling muscles and made a move to get her duffel.

"I got it," he said, reaching into the back seat.

They took two steps and then she stopped him. "You don't have to come in. Thanks for seeing me home, but..."

He stared down at her, so tall and broad that she fought the urge to wrap herself around him and shimmy him like a tree. "But what?" His voice was hoarse.

"But we can't see each other."

He simply looked at her and then straightened. Handing off the duffel, he started toward the driver's side. He opened the door. "See ya around, Tyler."

She almost gulped back a cry for him to stay.

Not to leave like this.

But it was best. They didn't have a romance — they'd slept together and only that once.

And he'd rescued her in a way. Or he'd led the team that had.

She threw a wave at him, and he ducked into the small car. "See ya, Hawk," she said quietly to herself and watched him back out, headed down the drive to the main road.

*****

The light knock on the bedroom door had Tyler sitting up, hair trailing over her face, staring blearily at her surroundings. Where was she?

Then her mind cleared as she focused on the high shelf where her twin sister's favorite stuffed animals had sat since she'd decided she was too old for them but couldn't part with the beloved and grubby toys.

Another knock and the door opened a little. Lexi popped her head around the frame. "Tyler?"

Tyler's heart brimmed over with love and affection for her sister. With her befuddling dream faded, she leaped off the bed and ran to yank Lexi into her arms. They hugged for a long minute, just feeling the familiarity of the person who shared a womb.

"Your hair's grown so much." Lexi spit out a mouthful and drew back, laughing.

Tyler grinned as she raked her gaze over Lexi. "You're dressed up. Where were you?"

She waved a hand, dismissing the full skirt she wore with a small retro print and the tiny T-shirt that barely skimmed her waist. "Just work."

"You never wore skirts to the flower shop before."

"Bo thought I'd look good in this style, and he was right, so I keep buying them in different colors and patterns. I've got to wear them somewhere, right?" Lexi's eyes, so like Tyler's own, danced with happiness.

But Tyler felt a punch to the gut at the mention of Bo. Hawk. Hawkeye, whatever. The man was a pain in her ass and she not only couldn't escape dreams of him but now her sister was bringing up his name.

"Well, you look great," she said to circumvent the topic of the man she wanted to forget. "And here I am all grimy from traveling all night."

"Sit down." Lexi pointed at her bed and Tyler sank to the mattress, already feeling the lull of sleep crashing over her again. This wasn't normal behavior for her. She had so much energy normally, and now she was battling against fatigue. Maybe it was just jet lag.

Lexi bounced down beside her and drew her slim legs up under her skirt. Reaching out, she brushed some dark reddish-brown hair from Tyler's shoulder. "You look a little tired. I'm sorry I woke you, but *Maman* said you were up here and I couldn't wait to see you."

Tyler smiled at her sister's characteristic enthusiasm for all things in life. The girl was a bundle of possibilities, and typically that rubbed off on Tyler. But all she wanted right now was her pillow and two more hours of sleep.

"I'm just tired from traveling," she said.

"*Maman* has invited the boys over and everyone is on their way. You don't want to sleep through your homecoming celebration, do you?"

She laughed. "No. I'll get up and shower. That will wake me up. And is that Cajun shrimp linguine I smell?" She took a deep breath and caught the notes of spice on the air.

"Yes, you're lucky. *Maman* only makes that for you. I'll pick out some clothes for you while you shower."

"Something comfortable. I can't even think of wearing a skirt right now." After what she'd been through, she just wanted leggings and an oversized T-shirt.

Lexi got off the bed and threw her a look as she strode to Tyler's closet, where she still had all her civilian clothes she hadn't worn in years. "I'll take care of you, sis. Go shower. And use my citrus amber body wash! It smells divine."

She chuckled as her sister's words followed her to the bathroom. Once behind the closed door, she didn't immediately turn on the shower, though. Instead, she looked in the mirror.

She rarely did this nowadays. Her life was training hard and training others harder. She didn't wear makeup or get to be the old Tyler often. Last time she'd gotten leave, she'd traveled to Washington DC to run the marathon instead of dolling up for some occasion.

Now, looking at herself, she felt like she wanted a bit of her old self back. She turned on the hot water and stripped off her clothes.

A glance in the mirror had her doing a double-take.

Was that a… *God, it is!*

Hawk had marked her with a red streak down the crest of one breast. Her skin prickled with remembrance of his beard stubble that had sprouted quickly in the baking Afghan heat. He'd run his jaw down over her, leaving kisses behind. Soft presses of his hard lips that had sent thrills all through her system.

Her nipples puckered, and she twisted from the mirror, not wanting to witness her own body's reactions to thoughts of Hawk.

Ugh, why did she have to sleep with him? Now she'd be faced with the man or talk of him, which would only make it harder for her to process and evict him from her personal life.

Harder now that she bore his mark.

She stepped into the shower and yanked the floral curtain shut. She almost laughed at the changes in décor in the bathroom. When they shared this bathroom with all their brothers, a simple blue utilitarian curtain had been all there was. Now Lexi had clearly spattered her love for all things flowery across the space in curtain, wall décor and even a fat pot on the sink holding three colorful Gerber daisies.

When she looked around the shower ledges, a giggle escaped. Leave it to her sister to have all the flowery scents on the market crammed into the shower. She read labels until she found the citrus amber one and squeezed some onto her palm. The smell *was* divine — it filled her nose and calmed her a bit.

She still didn't forget about the red mark, though.

After washing and standing under the spray for far too long, she began to hear bumping and thumping coming from downstairs that could only mean her huge brothers were home.

She stepped out of the shower and hurried through toweling off. Lexi had straightened her bed and laid an outfit there. She was relieved to see comfy shorts and one of her old favorite tops. The bright blue was the exact opposite of the grays, greens and blacks she wore on base. Just the pick-me-up she needed.

When she brushed her hair and reached for some of Lexi's makeup, she felt better. A little less fatigued, though it still lay deep in her like a dormant thing, ready to pounce. If she sat too long in one place, she'd probably nod off.

As soon as she set foot downstairs, her oldest brother Ben turned to her with a grin. Without a word, he scooped her up in his arms and lifted her off the floor so her feet dangled. She laughed and hugged him tight. Then was passed to the next brother and the next until she got into embracing their wives. The only one she didn't know very well was Chaz's wife Fleur. The lovely woman hugged her, though, and welcomed her home. When Fleur smiled at Tyler, she felt genuine affection shine through and then she stopped being worried about not knowing her new sister-in-law.

Lexi was in the dining room setting the table with their mother, who turned and came to hug Tyler once more.

She laughed. "You've already hugged me five times." She patted her *maman's* back.

"I know. I just want to get as many in as I can before you leave again." She stepped back and turned her attention to placing silverware alongside the dishes but Tyler knew she was hiding a tear or two.

Finally, Tyler went in search of her father. The man was home from work and enthroned in his chair with the evening news on but no chance at all of hearing it over the din.

Tyler padded over to his chair. He looked up, and she tipped over the chair into his lap like when she was a little girl.

"There's my wicked baby." He kissed the top of her head and drew her against his chest. She settled her head on his shoulder. "How are you, princess?"

He was one of the only people to treat her like a female and not a tomboy. Growing up it had been annoying and yet comforting at once. He knew her well enough to say she was both a strong female warrior and still a softy deep inside at times.

She mulled over his question. How was she? She could do the old "fine" routine, but her father would dig in and learn the truth.

In their private corner of the room, nobody could overhear their conversation.

82

"It wasn't easy, *Papa*." Her Creole came out most when she was emotional, and she could hear it in her drawl.

He squeezed her. "I'm sure it wasn't, honey. I've seen your brothers struggle as well at times."

Just speaking the words eased her a bit and she just snuggled for another long minute. When dinner was announced, she climbed off her father's lap.

And came eye-to-eye with Hawk.

When had he crept in? Who had invited the man?

He stared at her too deeply, probing her almost. She ran her fingers through her hair and turned for the dining room, ignoring his questioning gaze.

Are you okay? she could almost hear him asking.

Lexi had a bouquet laid across her place at the table and tied with a blue bow. Her favorite color that reminded her of a summer sky. Touched, Tyler lifted the flowers to her nose and inhaled deeply while hugging her sister with one arm.

As she lowered the flowers, she once again caught Hawk staring.

"Sit here by me, Bo," Lexi said, shooting a look up the table at someone.

Tyler followed her gaze and spotted the other member of the Knight Ops team, Rocko. A smile touched her lips and she shook her head. Things would never change. Since the moment her twin had set eyes on Rocko, she'd been trying to gain his attention. She had never said so, but Tyler suspected

Lexi had run off in hopes that Rocko followed her, but that didn't happen.

Hawk seated himself next to Lexi but that unfortunately put him at an angle from Tyler, giving him a perfect view of her.

She set aside the flowers she still held and avoided his stare.

"Before we dig into this wonderful linguine, I raise a toast," Tyler's father said from the head of the table. He lifted his glass of sweet tea that was probably doused with a trace of rum as his post-work cocktail.

She smiled at her father and raised her glass as well. They all did the same.

"To Tyler. Welcome home, princess. And to having this big family around us, healthy, safe and whole." Her father's words resounded inside her.

She might not have made it home from Kandahar. So many things could have gone sideways and then this wouldn't be a celebration. Now she knew the weight her brothers bore each time they walked out that door on a mission.

She sipped her own tea, feeling Hawk's eyes on her.

Dinner was as delicious as she remembered, and the conversations had everyone laughing nonstop. The little Knight children were the center of several of them, with her brothers relaying their escapades of fatherhood.

Tyler's heavy feeling of exhaustion was back, and she found herself slumping and wishing everyone would leave so she could slip away to bed. She propped her chin on her hand and stared at nothing.

When talk finally wrapped up, she went to help clear the table, but her sisters-in-law waved her off. So she stood in the living room wondering if anybody would notice if she went upstairs.

From the corner of her eyes she spied Hawk, looking her way, of course.

Yep, time to go before he could corner her.

Upstairs, she felt relief pour over her. The sensation left her perspiring and even more wiped out. She fell face-down on her bed, eyes shut.

Maybe she was coming down with something. She'd never felt such strange symptoms before.

The door burst open, and she rolled over to glare as Ben walked in unannounced and uninvited.

"Hawk sent me," he said by way of explanation when she narrowed her eyes at him.

"What? Why would he send you?"

"He was worried about you, and now I am too." He dropped to her bed, and her mattress sank low under his heavy muscle. His gaze drilled into her and she saw the man who led a special ops unit and not her big brother.

She scooted into a sitting position and wrapped her arms around her knees. "There's nothing to worry about."

"You're sleeping a lot."

"I'm jet-lagged."

"Or dealing with battle stress."

She didn't respond.

"You were pinned down for hours, fighting for your life. That takes a toll, Tyleri." His use of her nickname softened his words.

"Yeah, but we were fine. My unit pulled through. We didn't lose anybody though we were outnumbered. And just why the hell is Hawk sticking his nose in anyway?"

He arched a brow at her sudden outburst. "Could be he feels responsible for your well-being. He was the one to provide the backup your team needed."

"What else did he say?"

Ben cocked his head. "What should he have said? Is there something I should know?"

"No. The battle was over quickly."

He nodded. "Still, I think you need to see someone, Tyler. Talk it out."

"What, like a shrink?"

"We all need it at times. You can't do this job and not crack when you see or do something that goes against everything human you've been raised to know."

Once more, she saw in her mind's eye a man hitting the dirt, collapsing from the bullet she'd fired. Then five others after him.

"I can't talk to a stranger."

"Can you talk to me?" Ben asked.

"No."

"Who then?"

Her mouth opened and the name perched on her lips, but she wouldn't let herself say it. *Bo.*

When she didn't speak, Ben reached out and drew her into a hug. "Talk to Lexi then. Or those ugly fucking stuffed animals."

She giggled.

"Just talk to somebody, okay?" he said gruffly, and a wave of affection washed over her. She loved her brothers so much.

She nodded. "I will." It might be a lie. She wasn't sure yet.

Ben got up and made a face at her more befitting of a seven-year-old boy. She shook her head at his antics and lay back down. She closed her eyes but lay there for many minutes that turned into hours.

All her fatigue was still there, but now she couldn't sleep.

* * * * *

Bo hooked his knife into its guard on his ankle. Then he straightened and double-checked his gear. Colt M4A1 Carbine with SOPMOD kit, special issue to OFFSUS teams. A close quarter battle pistol, ENVG-B or enhanced night vision goggle-binoculars, gloves, a second knife and enough ammo to take down a small town.

Which might be the case, for all he knew. He hadn't yet received orders.

All this shit and no one to kiss goodbye.

He slammed his locker shut, ignoring the banter of Team Rou around him. With his cell phone in hand, he walked out of the room.

Texting Tyler probably was a bad idea. She'd made it clear she wasn't going to speak to him at all, even as friends over a big pot of linguine. Never before had he felt an urge to tell someone he cared for them before leaving on a mission, but that was before he'd had a beautiful, soft Knight woman in his arms.

What was there to say to her? *I was worried about you at dinner.* Or *I'm about to walk into some hell that none of us can guess at the outcome of. I just wanted to say…*

What? He didn't love her. Saying he cared about her sounded like a half-ass Hallmark card.

In the end, he withdrew his cell and thumbed out: *Hi Tyler. I'm heading out soon and I wanted to tell you. Maybe you understand why.*

To his shock, the little blip on the screen that told him she was writing a response appeared. His heart slammed faster as he waited.

I do understand.

Suddenly, he felt more bound to her than ever. She got him and he got her. He'd seen the post-battle stress on her like a cloak of despair and had sent Ben after her. He hoped her brother had been able to calm her spirit. Killing wasn't easy, and especially not your firsts.

We leave in a few, he texted.

Be safe.

Those two little words lifted a hope inside him that he wasn't too stupid to ignore. The woman wasn't just a one-night stand that he thought fondly back on. No, he wanted way more than the hot sex that came with Tyler Knight.

Tell me what you'll be doing today while I'm blasting away at freaks hiding behind trees in the swamps.

LOL. You're probably right about your mission. I promised Lexi I'd meet her for lunch but...

But what?

I didn't sleep well.

Dammit. Just as he feared. The woman needed to address the things digging at her or she would collapse under the weight. Or worse, she'd freeze when it came time to do it again.

Meet Lexi and then stop in at the base and talk to Pennywood. She's good at what she does.

Ugh, not you too.

Listen to me. I'm saying it because I care. Talk to Pennywood.

Have you talked to her?

Yeah, a few times.

And it had helped immensely, putting things into perspective and helping him to move forward.

The call came for transport, and he had to leave his personal belongings in his locker, and that included his cell phone. He dashed off one last text.

I want to see you when I come back.

IDK, Hawk.

Humor me. I'm about to walk into a nest of hornets armed with assault rifles.

Please watch yourself. I'll see you on the flip side.

He grinned and shut off his phone. As he strode back to his locker and stored the device on the top shelf, he replayed her words and their meaning. The tough little Marine wouldn't dream of dropping her armor, but her tough talk meant more to him than he could ever say.

Be safe. Watch yourself.

The words played in his head over and over. When had his orders... when he and Team Rou stormed a building and took fire... Tyler was in his head.

On his shoulder, urging him to watch himself.

In his heart.

Goddammit, he was going home and crushing his lips over hers one more time.

These assholes weren't taking him out. Not today.

Chapter Six

When Tyler drifted down the stairs, her *papa* looked up from his breakfast. He was dressed for work and had already made his way through his first cup of coffee and some toast. His smile was genuine.

"You're up early. Thought you'd sleep late."

She waved a hand. "I've been up since dawn. Habits are hard to break." She was normally up at daybreak and hit the ground running—literally. She was feeling sluggish from lack of exercise but she hadn't made time since coming home.

"Sit down and have some coffee."

"I think I'll pass."

He looked at her harder. "Then sit down and tell me what's wrong."

She'd always had a special bond with her *papa*. While her brothers loved to run home and kiss their mother, Tyler had always been a daddy's girl. And Lexi was the sweetheart of all family members.

She slipped into a chair and gave her father a direct look. "I'm having a hard time since..." She couldn't bring herself to say more. That she'd trained for combat, and just as she'd finally earned her combat action badge, she wasn't sleeping, having waking nightmares. What a laugh the universe was having on her of all people. She'd only been waiting to prove herself her entire life and now she was turning out to be a soft pudding of a woman.

As he set down his cup, he pierced her in his stare. "What are you going to do about it?"

"Ben thinks I should talk to the shrink."

"And you don't think that's a good idea." It wasn't a question—her *papa* knew her.

She shrugged. "It's an option that I haven't quite gotten to yet. I'd like to go to the cabin."

Concern creased his brow. "Alone?"

"Yeah. Just to think, to hear nothing for a while."

"You think being alone is a good idea?"

"*Papa*, I've been with people nonstop for years now. At basic training, on base, with family. I've thought a lot about this decision and I'm going."

He chuckled. "That's my Tyler—making up your mind with or without our blessing. Well, you have it. But you're going to promise to come right back in a day if you don't find the peace you're searching for. I can't have you out in the middle of nowhere with no way to communicate with us and feeling desperate."

She understood. Getting to her feet, she dropped a kiss to his shaven cheek and headed back upstairs to pack. As soon as she got her bag unzipped on her bed, her sister sat up in bed, hair wild and eyes only cracked.

"What are you doing?" Her voice was a wisp of its normal strength. "I don't have to be up for another hour."

"Lie back down and sleep then. I'll be quiet."

Lexi eyed the bag. "You're leaving?" Her tone rose in volume and an octave.

"Look, Lex, I'm going to the cabin. I need some time alone."

Eyes wide open now, Lexi swung her legs off the side of her bed. She wore only a cami and some tiny panties that looked like she was hoping to get laid. Tyler wondered when her naïve twin had morphed into a sex kitten. She also wondered what the hell Rocko was waiting for.

Lexi put her arms around Tyler, and touched by the gesture, she embraced her back. "I'll check on you, sis. I'm here for you."

Tyler nodded. When she drew back, she hid the tears swimming in her eyes and began to fold casualwear into her bag. Shorts, tops, workout clothes and some sweaters for cool nights.

"When will you be back?"

"A few days maybe."

"When are you expected on base?"

"A month." She winced. It seemed so long and not at all what she needed, though the military seemed to think after their ordeal, they deserved a long leave and time spent with family.

Lexi brightened. "Plenty of time to have girl time then. We can Christmas shop. You know I hate doing it alone."

Tyler gave her a smile and nodded. "Wouldn't miss it."

With plans laid and her bag packed, Tyler gave Lexi one last kiss and then went downstairs again to find her *maman*. This leave-taking would be harder. Her mother would encourage her to stay because she'd harbor similar fears as her father did. But Tyler knew herself very well, and this was what she needed.

When she broke the news to her *maman*, tears formed in the woman's eyes. She bore more lines on her face since Tyler had last been home. But no wonder with all her sons and one of her daughters off on dangerous work for the government. And Lexi was still a pain in the ass.

She hugged her mother tight and pressed her cheek against hers. "I'll be back soon. I just need a little reprieve. I want to listen to the loons and the water lapping the deck supports of the cabin and just think."

Her mother drew back and smiled, a sadness in her eyes. "You know that your spirit isn't much different from mine, honey. So while you might believe I'll be the toughest person to convince that you need time away, I'm actually the one who understands most."

94

Surprised, Tyler stared at her mother, whose beauty hadn't faded somehow even after raising all seven of them. "But you never leave. How do you do it?"

"Those times I've told you kids I'm going to visit my sister in Georgia?"

She gaped. "You were really at the cabin?"

She nodded.

"Does *papa* know?"

"Of course. We don't keep secrets, and he actually encouraged me to go. Now that you're all older, I just pick up when I need to and go."

"*Maman,* I love you for this." She threw her arms around her mom and kissed her soundly on the cheek. They hugged for a little longer.

Once Tyler was on the road with the window rolled down and the breeze threading its fingers through her hair, she let out a happy sigh. The drive wasn't a long one but the country was beautiful. She found the yellow-greens of the late season to be just as beautiful as the bright green of summer.

The wildlife she spotted reminded her of a game she and her siblings played on this very drive. They split into teams depending on who sat on the right or left of the vehicle. And those stuck in the middle were able to choose their team. Then whoever spotted the most animals would win and that meant they'd get to jump into the bayou first upon arrival.

Times like this she considered her life's plan. She wanted a family—always had. But she couldn't easily have one in her current position. However, she was young, she loved her work and wasn't ready to end it.

Her latest task in Kandahar might have given her a jolt to the system, but she had enjoyed aspects of it. Acting as a link between the military and their civilians and government had challenged her. Thinking on it, she'd return if asked, even if it meant reliving the battle that she was still processing.

The drive to the cabin didn't take long but the rest of the journey was more difficult. It involved parking the car and unearthing the pirogue boat from the underbrush as well as the paddle. She flipped the flat-bottomed boat over and set it into the water. With her bag settled safely so it didn't fall into the swamp, she dug the pole into the soft bottom of the waterway and pushed off.

Using her muscles felt good, and she craved more. It was time to end her period of laziness and get back to training because it made her happy.

When the cabin loomed before her, she stared with wide eyes. Her brothers had told her they'd built an addition, but she hadn't expected to find they'd doubled the size of the structure. With tall stilts holding the building out of the water and a deck that wrapped around all four sides, it was like something out of a vacation home advertisement. Throw in the new, bigger firepit of metal and stone and more lawn chairs she knew would be bolted down so the storms didn't blow them into the bayou and she could easily picture her big, growing family here all together.

Her father's old clunky grill he loved was still tucked against the side of the cabin and she laughed, thinking of all the times he manned it wielding a spatula and threatening to slap any boy who came near him. But he always allowed Tyler to come up and help him flip burgers or steaks or turn the shrimp skewers over before they burned.

She tied off the pirogue at the dock and tossed her bag onto the deck. Stepping foot on the weathered wood gave her a feeling of homecoming like nothing else had since returning to Louisiana.

She'd made the right choice in coming here.

Inside, she found more bedrooms added on and the living room extended. There was also a second bathroom, long overdue in her opinion.

After exploring, the first thing she wanted to do was strip off her clothes and jump into the bayou. She couldn't wait to propel herself through the water, pushing hard and fast and letting her mind clear.

* * * * *

The third shot hit its mark, directly over the previous two holes. Tyler reloaded and took her position, arm resting casually on her bent knee, eye to the scope.

A lapping sound filled her ears, but she tuned it out as she focused on her target. *Breathe in, out, in, hold.* She took the shot just as a canoe came into sight.

97

She eyed the person paddling it, not recognizing one of her brothers or even her *papa*.

It almost looked like... It appeared to be...

No. It can't be.

She got to her feet, weapon on safe, and watched the man approach.

Dammit, she'd thought about him far too much over the past two days spent here alone at the cabin, and somehow her thoughts had made him real. Hawk paddled up to the dock, his expression unreadable. He wore a crease between his brows yet his lips were soft as if he'd just blown out a sigh of relief.

"What the hell are you doing here?" she asked.

He skimmed his gaze over her as he reached out to grab the side of the dock and stabilize the canoe. "Is that your usual way to greet a man? Holding a weapon and swearing at him?"

She pushed out a short laugh. "I was training."

"At least you didn't shoot me on sight." He yanked the rope, firmly knotting the canoe to the dock and planted a big foot onto the deck. Suddenly, he was standing before her, as huge as ever and drawing her awareness to a graze on his temple.

"What the hell happened to you?" she asked.

His gaze traveled over her, and she felt the touch go straight to her pussy. Shit. They were all alone here and surrounded by water. Her only option was to outswim him or out-paddle him.

But she found herself setting down the weapon and then reaching upward, skimming her fingertips just below what could only be a graze left by a bullet. "Jesus, it was so close."

He caught her fingers in his hold and closed his hand tight, looking into her eyes. "I'm fine. It's you I'm worried about."

She searched those dark depths of his eyes and wondered why she was so breathless all of a sudden. "I'm fine too, as you can see."

He brought his other hand up to cup her cheek. Her eyes fluttered shut and when she opened them, he was even closer. His lips a breath away.

They threw themselves at each other. He hitched her against him hard, and she wrapped her arms around him, clinging. As he slanted his mouth across hers, she parted her lips and moaned at the feel of his tongue. He swiped it across hers until she grew dizzy and realized she'd forgotten to breathe.

Passion sweetened the bayou air, and now it smelled of soap and man — of Bo.

A sound broke from his chest and he lifted her off her feet as if she weighed ounces. In a few strides he reached the cabin door. He kicked it open and kicked it shut to keep out the worst of the mosquitoes. Then he took her straight to the nearest bed.

When he tore his mouth free long enough for her to speak, she gasped, "We can't do this."

"Oh yes, we fucking can." He slid his hand under her top and cradled her breast. She shivered at the way he took absolute control, as he seemed to do in every aspect of his life.

He pressed her back on the mattress and followed her down. The weight of his body on hers raised a gasp of pleasure to her lips—and she couldn't even swallow it down. Dammit, she was weaker than she wanted to be, especially when it came to this man.

His eyes were dark and piercing as he stared into hers. "Tell me plain. Are you all right?"

"Yes." She'd actually come to some terms with what she'd had to do back in Kandahar—for her country. In order to survive. Her mindset was improved, her heart less burdened.

"You're sleeping?"

"Yes." She was.

"Good, because you won't be tonight." With that, he lowered his head and captured her lips again. Held them prisoner for long, burning moments as he thrust his tongue against hers in a mimicry of what her hips were doing.

Damn traitorous hips, rising and falling on their own, seeking the huge erection she felt in his pants.

Need blossomed through her, and she reached for his shirt. As she yanked it over his head, he flashed a wolfish grin and slithered down her body to lay claim to her breasts.

100

In Kandahar, they hadn't had time for foreplay, but now she was experiencing firsthand just how damn good Hawk was at it.

He opened his mouth over the tip of her nipple and sucked through her tank top. She wore no bra, had no need here alone in the bayou. When the cloth was wet through and the extreme heat of his mouth met her flesh, she arched upward, grabbing at his short hair.

Each strong pull of his lips echoed through her. Then he changed angles.

The light scrape of hard teeth against her needy flesh ignited a fire in her that would never be doused after one night with this man and she knew it.

Dammit—times two.

He took her to a pinnacle of pleasure that never should be taking place from nipple play alone. The expert rotations of his tongue and the not-too-gentle nibbles had her crying out for more.

All right, she was begging. A girl like Tyler wasn't proud of begging for anything, yet she couldn't stop the soft pleas from leaving her lips if she tried.

"Take off my top. I need your mouth on my bare skin."

He cast a look at her that had her pussy throbbing. The man was hard steel against her thigh too—what was he waiting for?

101

She plunged a hand between their bodies and gripped his cock through his pants. The girth could scare a woman off, but she only gulped back a moan. She needed that inside her—every inch.

Pressing on his chest, she fought to move on top and take the joystick. He didn't budge, staring down at her, eyes hooded.

"I want to last, baby. And if you want me to as well, you'll take your hand off my cock."

She arched a brow and blatantly curled her fingers around his bulge.

A flick of his own brow told her two could play this game. It also left her worrying that he would be better at it.

He slid a hand under her top and cupped her breast. The callused feel of his finger stroking her hard, aching nipple was exquisite torture. She threw her head back and panted through the hum taking up residence in her core. He strummed the hard bud and then pinched it hard enough to make her cry out.

She dug her short nails into his biceps and began to rub his cock through his pants.

He rolled to the side as a way to make her release him. Pulling her with him, he lay her atop him with her shirt up and her breast aimed right at his hard lips.

She stopped dead, intrigued by the sight. Turned on by the eroticism of Hawk's mouth about to take her nipple into it. The tip strained toward his waiting lips. She leaned forward and brushed it across his mouth.

He groaned, and she took the chance to press her nipple into his open mouth. He clamped down on her with lips only. When the liquid heat of his tongue bathed her nipple, she trembled and could hold still no longer. She slung her thigh over his body, her pussy poised over his erection. The thin barrier of her shorts might as well be nonexistent, because she felt every single inch of his cock.

He sucked on her nipple and she ground down on him. Their shared groan filled the cabin. Suddenly, he whipped her top over her head, which sent her hair tumbling across her breasts.

Gently, he pressed her hair over her shoulder and drew her down to take her other nipple in his mouth. After five hot flicks of his tongue, she was wiggling faster and faster on him.

Heat licked at her insides, and she quaked for more. Those embarrassing pleas escaped her again. "Hawk, please. I need you inside me."

"Not yet." He tore his mouth free and began kissing down her torso, taking hold of her waist and moving her up so he could reach her navel, which he lapped with his tongue.

She dug her fingers into the pillow around his ears. She couldn't stand another second of this torture. Time to take what she wanted.

Needed.

She hurled herself off the side of the bed and reached for the waist of her shorts.

He looked at her, eyes dark with warning. "Once you take those off, there's no turning back, Tyler. You're mine all night."

Her mind raced. Muddled by lust, she might be missing something in his words, but she could find no loophole.

She hooked her thumbs in her waistband and in one shove, her shorts were gone.

His eyes darkened. "Leave the panties on."

* * * * *

He reached for Tyler. Her skin, silky beneath his rough hand, had his cock about to burst the confines of his skin. The minute he took off his clothes, it would be a race to the finish. He'd had too many days of needing her to go slow, and this time he was determined to taste her.

Savor her through her panties the way he had her breasts through her top.

Call it his fetish, though he'd never done it with other women. Tyler brought out a new secret pleasure in him that he wasn't shy about exploring.

Plus, she was wearing those cotton panties again, and this time they hugged her hips low and were a very sexy, very grownup midnight blue.

He tumbled her into bed with him again, covering her with his body so she couldn't escape. When he offered her a grin, she returned it.

"Game on," she whispered.

He chuckled. "We haven't even started, baby."

Kissing her was stealing all his control, but still he couldn't stop himself. As he slanted his mouth across hers for long, heated minutes, he willed himself to pull back. Still, he didn't.

He stroked her bare skin, teased her nipples until she was moaning, and then finally broke the kiss. "I've wanted nothing but this for days," he said raggedly.

Without speaking, she gripped his wrist and moved his hand over her torso, toward her pussy.

The damp cotton under his fingers ripped a groan from him. Watching her face, he eased his hand between her thighs and cupped her pussy. She went dead still, eyes burning with want.

As he began to glide his fingers over the crotch of her panties, feeling her swollen lips and the small bump of her clit, he battled to keep from stripping her and plunging inside. But no, he'd been dreaming of doing just this very thing and he wasn't about to stop now, even if his balls exploded with the pressure.

He trailed a fingertip over her seam to her clit. She sucked in a harsh breath and held it. When he rotated his finger around and around her sensitive nub that would be much more sensitive without her panties, she arched into his touch. Sliding his finger down again, he learned the outline of her. At the center of her, he pressed lightly. She moaned. He worked his finger deeper, so the cotton of her panties sank inside and grew wetter.

Growling, he moved down her body and opened his mouth over the crotch of her panties.

"You can… take them off." Her breath hitched.

"I plan to." Not yet. He sucked on her clit through the fabric and she came off the bed. He planted his hands on her hips to hold her in place, but she was strong and still managed to rut against his mouth. Her inner thighs tremored and small cries left her lungs.

The flavors seeping into his mouth were too much and he hooked a finger in the crotch, yanking aside the fabric to expose her wet folds.

To the air.

To his tongue.

He sank his tongue deep, and she cried out. His head flooded with her scents and taste, and he burrowed closer, unable to get enough.

As he drew circles over her slit, she dug her blunt nails into his shoulders. She was about to come apart, if her shaking told him anything.

"Oh. My. God. Hawk!" She rocked her hips, and he yanked her up to meet his tongue thrusts. On the third, she came apart under his mouth, in his arms.

Shudders racked her, and she twisted in his hold. He gentled the pressure of his tongue on her clit and brought her down slowly because he wanted to build her up all over again.

She loosened her grasp on his hair. The final pulsation faded beneath his tongue.

He raised his head and looked at her. "You screamed my name."

* * * * *

"That's what you say to me after that?" she rasped, still breathing hard. Her insides had melted, and she was still humming from the most explosive orgasm of her life.

His wicked grin said it all, but he spoke anyway. "I wanted to make you aware of whose name you just screamed."

He climbed off the bed and stood staring down at her, his cock bulging. As she looked on, he slowly licked his lips, wet with her juices, and even more slowly began to shuck his clothes.

She held her breath while each glorious, muscled inch was unveiled. She'd seen hot bodies but Hawk... She hated to admit it but he stole the prize.

Carved chest and abs rippling in a six-pack, or wait, was that eight? She skated her gaze down to the fat head of his erection distending his briefs. She sank her teeth into her lower lip.

He grunted as he slipped his hand into his briefs and drew out his cock.

Yep, just as impressive as she remembered, but last time she hadn't had time to explore him. She'd remedy that today. If she was going for it, she was all in.

The head of his shaft glistened with precum. He dropped his briefs and stepped up to the bed, fist clamped on his cock. Under his hand, his balls bulged.

She pushed onto one elbow and crooked a finger at him to come closer. He drew nearer the bed, and she looped her forearm around his hard ass, pulling him toward her lips.

"Not yet, baby." He moved away before she could swallow him. Then he stretched out next to her on the mattress and towed her into his arms. She tried to straddle him, aching to take that big cock, but he pinned her in place and kissed her.

The brush of his lips was tender. It raised something inside her, something she'd been missing out on. Something entirely girly.

She leaned into the kiss, giving stroke for stroke. He nibbled down to her jaw and continued on to her throat, swirling his tongue over her rapid pulse. She roamed her hand over his hard pecs and tested the sensitivity of his nipples. A faint moan was all she needed to pluck at his nipples more.

He was doing plenty of exploring too—he ran his hand over her breast and to her waist and then hip, kneading it. Unable to remain still, she bucked upward and parted her thighs for him.

The throb to be fucked by this man was driving her mad. She gasped as he took her nipple between his teeth and worried it lightly.

"Take me, Hawk."

"Don't worry, baby. You'll get what you need." He sucked on her nipple hard at the same time he thrust two fingers deep in her channel. She threw her head back on a cry and lost herself to the sensation of him probing her innermost spot. Juices flowed from her, and when he pressed up hard against the front wall of her pussy, the need hit a new high.

She locked a hand on his shoulder hard. He didn't relent on the pressure, held his fingers still and high right on... that... spot.

One small movement and she'd tip over the ledge again. A squeak escaped her, her body's drive for the breath she hadn't taken.

Hawk's gaze burned into hers. "Does that feel good, baby?"

She shook.

"Maybe if I move my finger like this."

He wiggled the tip of one and her insides started to flutter. She met his gaze, silently pleading for something she didn't even know was possible.

A volcanic eruption.

He brushed his lips across hers and began to hedge his fingers inside her, small thumps against her inner wall that blew her mind. She screamed as an orgasm tore through her. She yanked him in and kissed him with all the passion she was feeling in that moment.

He finger-fucked her fast and hard, drawing long, unearthly moans from her. He continued long after she went boneless, but it felt so good that she was already climbing again.

"You're fucking soaked." He drew his fingers free and painted her pussy with her juices. To her shock, he gathered more of her wetness and spread it over the tip of his cock.

Wild to get him inside her now, she grabbed him by the shoulders and threw him down, seating herself over his erection.

"Ty—"

She sank over him in one hard thrust.

"Jesus." His head lolled back.

She would have laughed if she wasn't ready to burst again. She cupped his jaw and claimed his lips in a long kiss that never seemed to end as she rose and fell on his cock. The angle was good but...

She rolled off and got onto her hands and knees. When he didn't move, she threw him a glance to find him kneeling behind her, his gaze locked on the globes of her ass.

"Fuck me, Hawk."

"You have the ass of a—"

"Runner?" she finished for him.

"Angel."

She shook her "angel" ass for him, hoping to entice him. It worked.

He locked his hands on her hips like twin vises and yanked her up and into him at the same time he gave a primal shove. He buried so deep that she let out a sharp cry. He went still.

"Did I hurt you?"

"Hell no. Move!"

His chuckle rumbled through her as he withdrew and slammed home again. The bed rocked, the headboard striking the wall. The friction of his cock inside her swollen walls was so good. Better than anything she'd ever had before, if she was honest. How many times could they get away with this and still walk away as friends?

Suddenly, she felt him falter. Then he picked up the pace. His balls swung into her body, slapping her clit. The wildness of the moment broke over her and she stiffened as he poured his cum into her body with fast jerks.

As he continued to pump his release into her, he slipped his arms under her and drew her up into his hold. Being in his arms in such an intimate pose with his mouth moving over her neck and soft, unintelligible words coming from his lips pulled a shiver from her.

111

He ground his cock deep one more time, cradling her jaw to twist her head to look back at him. His dark gaze smoldered. "I lost control. Don't ever tempt me like that again."

He flashed a grin and then kissed her.

Chapter Seven

Hawk woke to the feel of a warm, soft body plastered against him, and his hard cock knew what to do long before his mind caught up to the situation.

He slid home, buried in Tyler's wet sheath.

She moaned and roused from sleep too, reaching back to grab his hip. He anchored her against him and began to move. It only took three or four thrusts before he was fully awake and she was too.

Taking her from behind was hot as hell, but he wanted to see her face when she split apart.

He pulled out and gathered her in his arms.

"Bo..." Now when she was vulnerable from sleep, he was Bo, not Hawk. His heartstrings plucked, and he was far from surprised. Since the minute he'd seen her trying to storm over that wall back in Afghanistan, the woman had had a firm grip on him.

Gazing down into her sleep-fogged eyes, he brushed her hair from her cheek. "I want this to be slow."

She didn't speak, just leaned up to brush her lips over his and opened her legs. The gentleness of the gesture tightened his chest. He eased into her in one sweet stroke.

"Oh God," she murmured as he let out a groan. They began to move together, a slow melting of bodies and a finish ending in her tucked close and gasping out her pleasure.

Spent, he withdrew and skimmed his lips across her brow. "Sleep, baby."

"I was sleeping when you woke me," she murmured, eyes closed.

He chuckled. "I can't sleep next to you without wanting you."

But she was already asleep. He lay there for long minutes, too awake to drift off again. Besides, she was a conundrum that he was trying to puzzle out. Part warrior who demanded what she wanted — or took it. And part soft, sweet woman who accepted the attention he was more than willing to give. It was easy to come to the understand that she was both. He knew women enough to know they could do and be anything they wanted at any given moment. It was something he loved about the gender, and Tyler was the top of that list… and so much more.

Minutes passed with him easing back into sleep. Then she twisted in his arms to face him. He cradled her head to his chest and kissed her hair. She rubbed against his thigh.

The action roused him from whatever fog of sleep he was finally drifting into. Was she awake? He stole a peek and found her fast asleep. But she rubbed on him again.

Clearly her body was restless, seeking more.

Should he...?

The answer was a definite *yes*.

Disentangling himself from her hold, he moved down her body and parted her thighs. Her sweet pussy was glistening with need and their combined releases from earlier. Uncaring, he dipped his tongue to her folds.

He stifled a moan as his cock stretched. The urge to give her a huge orgasm with no strings attached took over. He spattered kisses and small licks up and down her seam. She moaned and stretched closer.

God, if he could wake her this way every morning of his life, he'd be a lucky man.

He lapped a circle around her clit before sucking on it gently. She came off the bed, awake and aware.

"God, Bo, don't stop."

Sliding his hands beneath her glorious ass, he feasted on her. Their combined flavors stimulated him more than he'd ever imagined.

"I need your fingers." She fisted the sheets.

He drove two high and deep as he sucked her pussy. She was so keyed up, so primed for him.

She came with a soft moan and a shudder. He pumped his fingers five more times, six, as he sucked on her hard pearl. When she collapsed to the mattress, almost asleep again, he raised his head and grinned to see her eyes wide and glassy.

"Go to sleep, love." He moved up the bed to take her in his arms again.

"Okay." She nestled against his chest. Did she have any idea that she'd done more than cuddle up to him? Tyler Knight had firmly ensconced herself in his heart.

He grinned against her hair. This could be war or peace, but either way, it was gonna be one hell of a ride.

* * * * *

Tyler walked through the door of the flower shop where Lexi worked and straight up to the counter. Nobody was around, but she knew her twin was working. She tapped a fingertip on the bell on the wooden top and it dinged loudly.

Nobody emerged from the back room. She tapped it again.

Nothing.

Impatient, she began to smack her hand off it a dozen times before Lexi appeared, looking ready to commit murder.

She stopped in her tracks. "It's you."

"Lexi. I need to talk to you."

"What are you doing here? I was just on the phone with Bo—"

116

She leaped around the counter and grabbed her sister by the upper arms. "I can't see Bo! He isn't on his way over, is he?"

"No, he just asked me to let him know if I saw you." Lexi widened her eyes as if Tyler had gone crazy and she was searching for a reason.

Tyler had—she'd lost her mind back in that swamp and slept with Hawk not once but repeatedly, which rendered it a relationship and not a loss of judgment. If only she'd been drunk, it would make things so much easier.

She shook Lexi by the shoulders. "You have to help me."

Her sister narrowed her eyes. "What did you *do*, sis?"

Glancing around to ensure nobody was in the shop, she whispered, "I made a mistake. A bad one. I can't see Hawk or talk to him. You have to tell him you never saw me."

Lexi was far from stupid and knew her brothers and sister better than anybody else on Earth. "Did you end up in bed with him?"

Oh God. The last thing she wanted to do was admit to the indiscretion. She shook her head. "I can't see him. You didn't tell him on the phone that I'm here, did you?"

She shook her head. "I didn't know who the maniac was out here ringing the bell."

"Good!" Relief trickled into her veins.

When she'd scooted out from under Hawk's heavy, muscled arm—okay, and threw one long, last look at his beautiful body—and then grabbed her stuff and hit the waterway, paddling her arms off, she had only thought to escape him at that moment. As soon as she'd gotten into her car, she realized she would never escape him. He was too close to her loved ones.

Lexi crossed the room and began filling a metal pail with water from a sink. While it filled, she went to a nearby display and began to pluck blooms into a bouquet.

"What are you doing? This isn't a time for work." Tyler strode up to her sister.

"I'm *at* work, sis. Didn't you realize? I'm pulling together a bouquet for a wedding shower. Oh that reminds me, Dahlia's preggers again."

She reeled at the change of topic. "Dahlia? Ben's wife?"

"Do you know any other Dahlia? Jeesh, this *is* the South, Tyler, and people are fond of naming their kids old-fashioned family names, but—" She skidded to a halt at the expression on Tyler's face.

"Lexi, what are you rambling about?"

"I need you to help me plan Dahlia's baby shower. Elise and the others asked me to rope you into it."

"But didn't we already throw her a baby shower with their daughter?"

"Yes, but this one's going to be a boy."

Her eyes goggled, and she blinked several times. "Is she far enough along to know this information?"

"No, I just have a feeling. Since you're here, you can help me choose some florals for the shower. There are soooo many beautiful blue flowers in season right now, and we're going to make this the best— Oh crap."

Tyler stared at her sister. "Oh crap? What's wrong now?"

"Bo's outside."

"Fuck!" She ducked around the counter and hunkered down. It was the most imbecilic move she'd ever made, but she was stressed and all she could think about was avoiding him at all costs.

The bell on the shop door rang and Lexi sang out, "Hi, Bo."

"Hey, Lexi. You said Tyler was here?"

That little shit. I'm going to break her arms for lying and saying she didn't tell Bo I was here.

Hidden by the big wooden counter, she crept toward the opening that led to the back room. With luck, her sister would occupy Bo enough to allow her time to escape.

Moving slowly, she threw a look toward the counter and thankfully did not find the man staring down at her. She beelined it for the darkness of the back room and straightened to her full height, searching for an exit. If she was cornered back here, she was going to be pissed.

But fate came to her rescue, and she grabbed a door handle. When she pushed it open, a fire alarm sounded.

Of course, what else could happen? She hurried up and slammed the door shut, but the bell continued to blare. Let Lexi deal with the authorities who would show up to see who was robbing the flower shop. Tyler took off running, zipping around the block to her car. Damn if Bo wasn't parked behind her, his black jeep nearly booted up against her own little car like a dog ready to mate.

Visions of urging him to take her from behind so he could be ohhh, so deep spread like honey over her senses. No time to think on the things she should be regretting. She hopped behind the wheel and gunned it out of the parking spot.

The city was decked for Christmas with greenery and white twinkle lights, but she didn't have time to appreciate the season change she loved in her hometown. She was too busy making a getaway and wondering how she could possibly keep this up. Sooner or later she and Hawk would be in the same room at a family event. Then what?

She imagined the man flower-shopping with Lexi for the baby shower while spilling the beans about what had taken place in the cabin. She shook her head. Lexi would go into romance mode and play matchmaker and that was the last thing Tyler needed.

She glanced in the rearview mirror and nearly choked on her own tongue. Coughing, she looked twice.

The black jeep. No way was this coincidence.

When it pulled up beside her in the left turn lane, she pivoted her head away. A horn blasted. The light turned green and she shot ahead, leaving Hawk behind, unable to get out of his lane to follow.

A small victory that she didn't feel. This was childish, and Tyler was a level-headed woman. She needed to face this thing head-on and eye to eye.

Ahead, she spotted a place to pull off. She did so and waited, counting forty seconds before the black jeep drove in behind her. Bo got out, dressed in all black and looking ready to kill.

She shuddered but not with fear — with longing to feel that big, hard body against hers again.

Nope. She was finished with this momentary insanity that had taken over her brain and libido ever since Kandahar. She had to get a grip — now.

She got out and faced him.

His dark eyes drilled into her. "You left."

"It was for the best."

"Without saying goodbye."

"I didn't want to wake you."

His eyes bulged and a muscle fluttered in the crease of his jaw, showing he was obviously grinding his teeth. "Woman." His tone held a warning that instantly aroused her anger.

Folding her arms, she bit off, "Don't speak to me like I belong to you."

"I'd never say any woman belongs to me." He grabbed her by the arm and steered her to the door of a pub. New Orleans was overflowing with small joints like this and it was unlikely any of her brothers would be in here, but the moment her feet crossed the threshold, she cast a look around the room for them.

There was no Ben sipping away at a beer. No Chaz hanging with a buddy between Knight Ops missions.

She dragged in a deep breath but squeaked with surprise as Bo hauled her to a booth and crowded in next to her so she couldn't escape. Being barricaded by his warm body made her slump down in the booth.

She wanted him.

She didn't suppose he'd accept her dragging him into the ladies' room to have sex in a stall would do for an apology. It definitely wouldn't work in her favor when she tried to convince them what they'd done was a mistake either.

Besides, the bathroom had to be disgusting.

She chewed her lip as he glared at her, body angled toward her.

"Wait a minute. Don't move." He got up and stomped to the bar. When he came back with two shots of amber liquid and slammed them down in front of her, she eyeballed him.

She picked up a shot in each hand and hammered them back, one after another, before he could think to gape at her.

"What did you just do?"

"Thanks for the shots."

"You're crazier than I expected, and damn if I'm not a little turned on right now knowing you can put away that much alcohol without flinching. But I'm not against throwing you over my shoulder and carrying you out of here either if you pass out."

She wouldn't pass out. "What do you want, Hawk?"

He shifted his jaw so it bulged, looking more square and manly too, dammit. "I like a strong woman, Tyler."

"You can just forget about—" She clamped off the thought, realizing what he'd said. Was he telling her that he liked and appreciated how she was, exactly as she was?

"But not a stubborn one," he concluded.

There it was—the other boot dropped.

They stared at each other.

"I'm not stubborn." Now she sounded like it and hated herself.

He arched a dark brow. "That's why you won't admit that something happened back in that cabin."

"It was just sex," she said a bit too loudly. Two guys at the bar looked at them.

"That was not just sex," Hawk said evenly. His words directed her attention to his mouth, which she remembered far too well—between her thighs in the middle of the night.

She reinforced her determination. "We can't discuss this anymore. It was a bad idea to sleep together. It complicates everything, and you can't deny that."

"No, I can't. I don't relish the idea of telling your brothers, but I'm prepared for punches if it comes to that."

"You can't tell my brothers! God, what are you thinking?" she practically yelled.

The men pinning down the barstools eyed her again.

She lowered her voice. "Look, I have to get home and apparently there's some baby shower Lexi needs me to help plan. Plus it's the holidays. I'd like to spend some time with my family before I have to return to my duties. Can we just forget about this?"

"No. We can't, Tyler."

She didn't like how controlled he was, not one bit. She opened her mouth to say so, but Hawk scooted from the booth and stood staring at her. "It wasn't just sex. It wasn't just a one-time thing and you know it. If we were alone, you'd be in my arms and I'd have you locked to that wall over there fucking you. But since you're far too stubborn to admit it, I'll just go and you can think on it for a while."

The vision of him pinning her to a wall and fucking her took over her brain, and by the time she emerged from the fantasy, Hawk had walked away. She scrambled from the booth as the door closed behind him.

She shook herself. What a damn mess she'd gotten herself into, and now to top it off, the double shots were hitting her system and she was too woozy to call herself anything but a lightweight drunk.

She settled in the booth again and dropped her head into her hands.

* * * * *

"Heyyyy," Ben drawled as he entered the club. Hawk stood to greet him. Team Rou was already here, but Ben was the first of Knight Ops to show up for Hawk's offer to get together for a round of holiday cheer.

The big table had been set up to accommodate the whole crew, and Hawk expected a rowdy night ahead. He hoped it took his mind off one little saucy, stubborn woman, but he doubted it. He hadn't seen or heard from Tyler in a week, and he'd gone from wanting to storm into her house and demand more from her and dropping all hope of more than her stubborn sass.

He wanted a relationship, goddammit. That was pissing him off more than anything. He finally, after all this time, had found a woman worthy of pursuing and she was refusing him at every turn.

Except in bed. She couldn't deny him then. *Hmm... Maybe —*

Ben clapped him on the shoulder and then noticed the blue half-moons that hadn't even begun to fade on his biceps, left there by Ben's own little hellcat sister.

"Whoa, dude, I see you've been getting some action. Who was she?" Ben chuckled and took a seat. Luckily the chairs here were heavy enough to hold the men, who were far from average-sized.

Hawk rubbed a finger along his nose, wondering how to respond to Ben. He was more than willing to take the punches Ben was sure to dole out — if Tyler gave him something to fight for. But at this moment, Hawk wasn't so damn sure.

"Someone worth it, I hope," Ben said.

He nodded and waved for the waitress. She came bearing pitchers of beer and some appetizers, spreading them along the table. At that moment, Tyler's brothers Sean and Chaz entered with Roades, Dylan and Rocko behind. Team Rou all rose to their feet and there was a lot of clapping on backs and fist bumping.

"This is a good idea, Hawk. Thanks for the invite. We never get together like this," Dylan said.

"Because we're always tied up in—" Hawk was cut off by a chorus of, "Fuckin' Mississippi."

"Hey, what do you got against the whole state? Just because you had a few bad encounters there," Hawk started.

"Not a few. Dozens," Sean said.

"To be fair, it's just that one county," Ben added.

Laughter sounded down the table and then they dug into their snacks and beer. When the pizza arrived in steaming pies piled high with meat, Hawk sat back and observed Tyler's family members.

He'd spent years working alongside them or in some way connected through the agency they worked for. But now he was truly looking at them and wondering how they would act as brothers-in-law.

The camaraderie within a team always brought on merciless ribbing and name-calling. They were also fiercely protective of their sisters. Usually Lexi was the focus of their big brother bodyguard, and they didn't say much about her throwing herself at their fellow teammate Rocko.

So far Tyler had flown under the radar. What if he suddenly announced they were sleeping together? Things could swing either way.

If only the woman would give him some indication she wanted more. But her silence was deafening.

He pushed out a heavy sigh.

"Man, looks like you were with a hellion." Sean pointed to his arm and the bruises Tyler had left there.

He smiled. "Yeah."

"I'm surprised you would pull yourself away long enough to buy us pizza and beer."

"Yeah, well, she hasn't wanted to see me in a few days."

Several conversations paused and the men looked at him. "Maybe you couldn't keep up with her," Rocko quipped from farther down the table.

"I don't think that's the case. You guys ever run across a woman who runs scared?"

All five of the Knight brothers nodded.

Hawk laughed. "What is this? A type you all have?"

They exchanged looks. "Seems to be the case. Every one of us had to convince our ladies at some point that we could make things work," Ben said.

Hawk's mind flipped over that tidbit. Actually, it was a delicious morsel of information. If they liked the chase and capture with their wives, maybe Tyler was the same?

Chaz elbowed him and poured him another glass of beer. "Have a drink, bro. Don't overthink things. If she's meant to be yours, she will be."

That was his problem—he knew women well, very well, and did tend to dwell on their mindsets. Hell, he'd done it with his ex-wife Elise for months before finally deciding things weren't working out between them, that the relationship lacked the passion despite them being best friends.

Luckily, she'd agreed and brought up the subject first. Thing was, he'd spent more time thinking about Tyler and trying to figure her out than Elise and any of his past lovers put together.

That had to say something.

He lifted his beer glass. "To women and the crazy bastards who love them."

They all clinked glasses and chorused his sentiment.

After taking a big gulp, Ben gave him a nod and got up to leave. "Speaking of the woman... I've gotta hit the road. Something with Dahlia's father."

"Oooh. Say hello to Colonel Jackson for us," Sean quipped.

"He's not Colonel Jackson when he sees his granddaughter. One look at her big brown eyes and he's Grandpa." Ben grinned and threw a last wave. "See ya tomorrow, Hawk?"

He straightened in his chair. "What?"

"Family dinner, something our mother's roped us into. She's trying to squeeze in as much as possible while Tyler's home, I think."

His heart gave a hard thud at her name — and the thought that she wouldn't be in Louisiana for long. He nodded. "I'll be there."

Chapter Eight

Tyler pulled out the shopping list Lexi had thrust into her hand, telling her to pick up a few things for this party.

"But why are we having another family party?" Tyler usually didn't mind shopping, but she'd gone so long without it that she couldn't imagine owning a new skirt would improve her life. Yet there it was right there on the list, written in Lexi's flowing hand.

New skirt. Make it sequins. And short. Your legs are great, sis.

She sighed and stuffed the list back into her pocket. Besides a skirt, she was meant to pick up some more white cloth napkins and gold charger plates. Since the family had grown since the previous year, *Maman* needed more for her matching table-scape.

"Ugh. Table-scapes and sequin skirts. What has my life come to?" she muttered as she crossed the parking lot of the shopping center, angled for the party store.

When she walked inside, "Jingle Bell Rock" filled her ears and the smell of Christmas surrounded her. Cinnamon pinecones in glass bowls and net bags, ready for somebody to carry home for their own table-scape. Whatever the hell that was anyway. Give her an automatic weapon and she could handle it, but the party store was freaking her out already.

She grabbed a shopping basket and started searching aisles. After battling to get past an angry mother with a screaming toddler in the shopping cart, Tyler made it to the front counter and asked for the things she needed. Five minutes later, she had napkins and extra gold chargers—she picked up a dozen in the event all five of her sisters-in-law were expecting. This way they'd have them for next year.

With a big bag with rope handles clutched in her hand, she made her way down the sidewalk toward the next shop, a gadget and tech store. Here she bought all her brothers the junk people put in stockings, but this year she wasn't going all out with gifts and wrapping. She had other things occupying her mind.

Like Hawk.

Why the hell had she given in to him a second time? She hadn't been distraught like the first time, wanting human comfort from somebody familiar to her. No, she'd slept with the man because she'd wanted to.

If she was honest, she wanted to again.

Luckily, he hadn't come around the house. She'd been living in fear of that for days. Her interfering sister and her *maman* would know exactly what was going on after one look at Tyler's face. She couldn't have that.

Burdened with two heavy bags, she hit the body care store and grabbed gift sets for all the ladies in her family. Plus some baby-friendly crap for the niece and nephew. She walked all the way back to her car to unload the bags in the trunk before heading on with her errands.

She took out the list and stared at it. Lexi wanted what? Chocolates? Now that she could do.

She spent the longest time in the sweet store, choosing pounds as a family gift to all on Christmas Eve and grabbing a small bag of chocolate-covered pretzels for herself. When she reached the checkout, she took one look at the impulse buys there and was snagged.

At least that was what she told herself after picking up an oversized pecan cluster in a simple black box for Hawk.

She pushed the questions to the back of her mind and shoved her hormones firmly down, paid for her items and left the shop.

With Lexi taken care of, she was free to do her own shopping. Her sister would be sad to learn there was not a sequin skirt in Tyler's future, but there was a faux leather mini in black with a belt tie. She could think of a dozen shirts in her closet to wear with it, and she'd get far more mileage from the faux leather. Besides, she wasn't into impersonating a disco ball.

Feeling satisfied, she wove through the store and stopped dead in her tracks as she spotted the big man browsing women's lingerie. Hardly breathing, she stared at his back and then down to his hand, so familiar because of how many times she'd felt it on her body. Those long fingers slid hangers aside and inspected frilly and see-through nighties.

For a heartbeat, she wondered why the hell he'd think it was okay to buy her lingerie.

Then she realized it might not be for her.

A flush climbed her neck and face, and she twisted away but not before he turned.

Even with her head down and her quick move to flee, he caught her by the elbow. He spun her to face him, a grin on his face that caused her heart to do a tango.

"Uh, Hawk. What are you doing here? Shopping for your um, sister?" She slid a look past him to the rack of blush-colored robes that wouldn't conceal the invisible woman.

He gave her a flat look that said he wasn't remotely amused.

She pulled free of his hold, mostly because the heat sinking into her flesh was starting to make her mind go blank. She straightened her shoulders and met his eyes.

Mistake. Huge mistake. What she saw there had her nipples hardening.

"You haven't called me," he ground out.

She blinked. "You made it pretty clear at the pub that you were finished talking."

He dropped his stare over her, and she practically felt him plucking at her nipples with those dark eyes of his.

Fighting for control, she released a slow breath. "I need to get home. Nice running into you."

She could think of nicer ways to spend time with the man. Like underneath him.

Walk calmly to the checkout and pay for the skirt.

She threw him a small wave and turned to go.

"Tyler."

Her heart squeezed. Dammit, there was a plea in his voice.

She pivoted.

He approached slowly, muscles rolling with each step he took. When he plucked the skirt from her hands, surprise had her mouth gaping open.

"I'm buying that."

"No, I'm buying it. And we're accessorizing." He grasped her elbow again and led her to a wall of shoes and jewelry. When he took down a pair of black tights and some booties, she stared at him.

"How do you know my size?"

He arched a brow. "I've touched you, remember?" He leaned closer. "All. Over."

Oh God.

"Fine, I'll get these but I have tops at home. I'd like to just leave."

But Hawk seemed intent on dressing her. She felt like Ken had raided Barbie's closet and was happy to help her with a makeover, except Barbie was content to wear sweats and a T-shirt if it meant attracting less of his attention.

He pulled her through racks of tops until he located a simple red one with a small V-neck.

"Won't I look like a hooker? Red and black leather?"

"You question my taste level? Trust me. Nothing is revealing about this outfit, but it is festive. Perfect for the party."

"Wait—you know about the party?" That meant he'd been invited.

"Not a party really. More of a gathering." He shrugged a massive shoulder, reminding her how out of place the huge special task force dude looked in a women's clothing store.

And how many women were staring at him as if hoping to get him in their Christmas stockings.

Somehow, they ended back in the lingerie section in front of a circular display of tiny panties.

"This is where I draw the line at you dressing me. I'm not wearing those."

He reached for a gold pair with jewelry on the butt crack.

"Hell no."

"It's all right. I prefer the cotton briefs on an athletic woman like yourself anyway."

Which made her perversely wonder if he wouldn't think her sexy enough for the gold ones. She shot a look at them and then shoved the thought firmly from her mind. She was not getting roped into buying things she'd never wear based on his interest.

Besides, she didn't want Hawk.

Her nipples screamed, Yes, we do!

She glared when he chose several slinky items that would feel like she was wearing dental floss and put the entire lot into the fitting room.

Tyler came to a standstill. "I'm not trying those things on."

He stepped up to her, so close that his big chest brushed against her needy nipples. She stopped breathing as he ducked his head, mouth close to her ear. "Be a good girl and try them on."

"No." She tried for firm and got shivery. Damn her body — why couldn't it cooperate?

Before she guessed his intention, he walked her back through the fitting room door and followed her inside. The cubicle was insanely small when you added a huge hulk of a Marine in it with her, and she was crammed into a corner.

He reached for her. The instant his callused hands touched skin, her libido was off the charts. He slammed his mouth over hers, tongue invading, seeking. She moaned and he swallowed the sound, sealing off any more with his kiss.

She stood helpless, fighting the urge—no, need—to cling to him and succumb to every dirty wish the man ever had.

He peeled off her top and went for her jeans. As he broke the kiss and began to suck on her neck, he somehow managed to get one of the lacy camisoles on her. Drawing back, he raked his gaze over her. She glanced down to see he'd also removed her bra and her hard nipples were distending the lace.

"Now. About you wanting me." His low voice washed over her like warm liquid.

"I... never said I wanted you."

"I can see you do." He plunged his fingers into her panties and found her seam slick and her clit swollen. Her hips rocked without permission from her brain, and she slid her pussy right over Hawk's fingers.

"Oh God," she rasped.

"Shhh." The way he crooned against her lips had her gasping and opening her mouth for his tongue again. He plunged inside, sweeping the interior as he began to finger her up against the wall of the cubicle.

She parted her thighs to give him better access, and he took immediate advantage by driving a finger into her pussy.

She trembled in his hold and kissed him back with all the desire she'd been feeling for days now.

The pressure of his fingers coupled with the forbidden action of being fingered in a ladies' dressing room by a big delicious man had her peaking in seconds.

The orgasm struck hard and fast, yanking her world sideways.

"That's it. Fuck yesss," Bo whispered in her ear as he rubbed her clit with his thumb and thrust his finger through her pulsating walls. Her knees went out and he supported her, holding her through the last aftershocks.

She got her feet under her long enough to straighten up.

He removed his hand from her panties and stood back. With a wink, he stuck his finger in his mouth and sucked it clean.

Another tremor hit her, and she wrapped her arms around herself.

The gleam in his eyes was wicked. "I've got these and I'll deliver the package today early enough that you can get dressed for the party."

She pushed out an uneven breath. "Thought you said it was more of a gathering."

He grinned and took up the items she'd been prepared to buy. "On second thought, I don't like the cami you have on. Maybe the black…"

Before she could respond, he left the fitting room, leaving her standing there alone and still shaking from her orgasm.

Hawk had won that round, but now she knew enough not to get caught alone with him.

Except they hadn't been alone at all. The man had just finger-fucked her in a store.

And it was the hottest thing ever.

She hurriedly got out of the cami and back into her street clothes. When she stepped out and didn't see him, she searched the store and didn't find him.

Dammit, he'd made an escape before she could find the gumption to tell him off for being so...

Highhanded, that was the word.

Daring was another than came to mind.

Whatever she called him, her body knew just what to do each time Hawk came within an inch of her. Now if she could just make her mind will away these feelings of heart-leaping happiness each time she set eyes on him, she'd be all set.

* * * * *

That was the second time Hawk had given Tyler pleasure without taking any for himself. He was glad to do it—wanted to many, many more times. But he also was bursting with lust.

The way she'd ridden his fingers in the fitting room and then come apart for him, shattering on his fingers and soaking him.

He ran his finger under his nose again, smelling her on his skin. Fresh and light. God, how was he

139

ever going to make it hours before going over there and finding a way to take her again before, during and after the party?

Leaving the bag of things he'd purchased for her on the floor by the door of his apartment, he walked straight to the kitchen and got himself a glass of cold water. The chill did nothing for his burning desire, though. He finished every last drop and set the glass into the sink.

When his cell buzzed, he made a grab for it. Maybe it was Tyler asking him to come over. Or meet her. Or—

Dammit, it was Colonel Jackson.

"Get your ass down here in ten, Hawk."

"Sir, it takes me fifteen in traffic."

"Ten," he reiterated.

The hairs on the back of Hawk's neck stood up. Even though the colonel was known for being a hard-ass, it must be crucial if he was being so demanding.

"Ten," Hawk agreed and ended the call.

He strode to his room and quickly changed to the black cargo pants and T-shirt that would carry him through whatever bullshit mission he was being sent on.

And on the night of the Knights' party.

"Fuck."

With his gun strapped in place, he grabbed his keys and headed out the door. On second thought, he backtracked and picked up the bag of clothes. If he really was being sent into the swamps to hunt down some idiot threatening their homeland, then maybe he could get one of the peons of OFFSUS to deliver the bag to Tyler.

It took eleven minutes for him to reach the base, but Jackson didn't seem to be counting. As soon as he arrived and saw Team Rou sitting around or leaning against the walls, he knew he was never making it to that party.

He wasn't going to see Tyler again tonight.

He pushed out a sigh and took his orders with a sharp salute. On the way to the black SUV Depeux was driving to their destination, he strode to his jeep and fetched the bag. He carried it to one of the men guarding the gate and handed it to him. With a word or two, the errand was passed off.

When he got into the passenger seat of the SUV, Depeux threw him a look. "What was that about? You got him a gift?"

"Yeah, asshole."

"You're in a bad mood. Did you have to pull your dick out of some hottie to come here? I'd be ticked off too." Depeux glanced in the rearview mirror. "Everybody buckled?" he asked in a high-pitched tone of a Southern momma. "Now y'all keep your shoes on, you hear? And no potty breaks—I told ya to go before we left."

The guys all laughed, but Hawk wasn't feeling it.

"Damn, you're really ticked. What the hell happened?" Depeux asked.

"Missing a party tonight."

"Oh. Important one?"

"Important to me."

"Family?"

He thought about it. "Sorta." If he could only figure out how to make Tyler his, then the men he loved as brothers would become his own family. Not to mention how protective he already felt for Tyler's twin sister.

Silence sounded for several minutes. Then Depeux said, "Does this have anything to do with Tyler Knight?"

Hawk wasn't into playing games, and there was no reason to deny it anyway. "Yeah. I fucking want her."

One of the guys blew out a low whistle. "I wouldn't fuck with a Knight sister for anything. I like my teeth and balls too much."

Everyone laughed but Hawk.

"Well, I'm pretty sure I can handle myself against the Knight boys."

"That's true — it's Tyler you've gotta watch out for. That chick is hardcore."

He imagined her coming apart for him in the fitting room, wearing red lace, the sexiest woman alive. "It's what I love about her."

"Love? Man, you've gotta focus on this mission. We can't have our fearless leader distracted by a pretty piece," Depeux said.

"I'm good to go." He was. He was just feeling the weight of not seeing her tonight in the outfit they'd shopped for together. Of not sitting next to Tyler at the big family table and watching her smile and joke with her loved ones.

If he even won her over and made her his, how could they even add to the family? He wanted a family with her and with both of their jobs, it wasn't exactly a possibility. If they had kids, they'd be raised by family—her *maman* or Lexi or even his own sister.

No life for a child to be brought into. If he had kids, he'd raise them himself, and he wanted his wife by his side for it.

He scrubbed a hand over his face and watched the miles slip by out the window. His thoughts were irrelevant, because right now, he couldn't even convince the woman he loved to give them a chance.

Then again, he hadn't come right out and asked either.

* * * * *

"Tyler, who was at the door?" Lexi sang out as she entered the living room.

In shock, Tyler turned from the door, bag in hand.

"What is that?" Lexi came forward.

143

She couldn't believe it—Hawk wasn't coming. He'd sent a carrier to deliver the bag of clothes he'd bought her to wear tonight. Disappointment was a concrete block she couldn't swallow and lodged heavily in her throat.

"Tyler?" Seeing her distress, Lexi took her by the upper arms. "What is it?"

"Lexi, I can't do this party thing. I've got to get out of here."

"Get out of here?"

She shoved the bag at her sister. "Yes, I need air. This is too... too much." She waved at the house that was decked from top to bottom, inside and out with gold tinsel, Santa figurines and mistletoe. The dining table had an extension and looked ready for the Queen of England to come for dinner with all the gold and white on it as well as a massive floral centerpiece Lexi had made herself of white roses, gold bells and holly.

Tyler grabbed her coat off the peg and checked the pocket for car keys. "I'll be back in a few days, Lex." She leaned in and planted a kiss on her stunned twin's cheek.

"Wait! A few days? You're not staying tonight? It's just a family gathering, Tyler. Nothing to be freaked about."

"It's not that."

"Then what is it?"

She shook her head, heart cracking at the disappointment she'd put on her twin's face. She wanted Lexi to be happy, but she had her own life to sort out, and first and foremost was getting over Hawk.

The man had somehow wiggled his way into her heart and stolen her ability to think of him as a simple man, a fellow special ops leader or a friend of her family.

Tears flooded her eyes.

Lexi grabbed her and pulled her into a hug, pressing her face against Tyler's hair. "Love you, sis. I'll make sure our parents understand. Be safe. Promise me."

"I will. I just need to think on some things."

Lexi drew away, searching her face for signs of distress. Whatever she saw convinced her to release Tyler. She stepped to the door and left.

The drive to the cabin was a hard one, because tears kept threatening and that lump in her throat wouldn't go away. Why was she acting like this? What she needed was to get back to her job on base. Training others, beating her personal record, that was all she needed for a happy life.

Except now it wasn't. Not at all.

The Christmas wonderland lining the streets of New Orleans thinned out to the suburbs with red ribbons and wreaths on front doors. Then to the country, where the occasional fence corralling horses would bear a Happy Holidays sign.

When she reached the bayou, she parked the car and considered what she'd run away from.

Not from Bo or her family but from her own feelings. When had she become such a coward? It wasn't back in Kandahar—her emotions then had come and gone, were dealt with.

What she felt for Bo had not gone, though. And somehow, she had to come to terms with moving on without him in her life, popping up in her rearview mirror and forcing her into pubs or fitting rooms.

Fact was, she wanted him there tonight, sharing in her family's festivities, even if it was weeks before Christmas. She wanted to wear the outfit he'd picked out for her and see the appreciation glimmer in his dark eyes.

When was the last time she'd wanted something for herself? The decision she'd made years before to run off and join the Marines had been the last thing she'd really done for herself—the rest had been for her country or to make her family proud.

She wanted Bo, dammit.

She got out of the car and before she closed the door, she spotted a crate in the back seat filled with decorations Lexi had either forgotten or had some other intention for. Knowing her sister, she'd planned to decorate an orphanage or something while singing Christmas carols and tossing lollipops to all.

A smile tugged at her lips and she reached into the back seat for the crate.

Chapter Nine

Hawk paddled through the dark waters of the bayou. Navigating at night didn't bother him, and he wasn't a bit squeamish when a snake fell off a tree branch into the bottom of the boat.

Without switching on a light, he pinched it behind the head and tossed it overboard. The splash echoed in the still swamp.

When he rounded a bend in the waterway, the lights came into view. He started at the sight of the Knights' cabin decked out in twinkle lights. She'd been busy, even if she did have a few days to do it in.

After wrapping up Team Rou's mission, Hawk had banged on the Knights' door at midnight and asked to see Tyler. Her father had shaken his head and mumbled she'd gone to the cabin.

On his drive here, Hawk had pictured many scenarios, but none of them ended with him finding her Christmas spirit coming forth here in the middle of nowhere and all for her own benefit.

The dozen other cases had included her experiencing deep depression or a hardcore case of PTSD and taking target practice on swamp creatures.

It had also involved a fleeting thought that Tyler had learned he wouldn't be at the party several nights ago and been disappointed enough to disappear.

That thought he'd shaken off. She hadn't been happy to learn he was invited to that party. Though he was ticked that he'd missed it. He'd wanted to see her strut her stuff in that little black skirt. Of course, he never would have been able to keep his hands off her, and her brothers would have seen. Which would have ended in a holiday brawl to go down in the history books.

He let out a heavy sigh and drew up to the cabin's dock. After roping off the canoe, he grabbed his duffel and crossed the deck to the door. When he rapped softly, the door whipped open and he was greeted by the barrel of a gun.

"Back off, asshole," Tyler bit off.

"Baby, it's me, Hawk."

Silence reigned and then she lowered the weapon and stepped back. "What the hell are you doing here?" She dragged her fingers through her loose hair. Behind her, all the light in the entire cabin was a single candle.

He dropped his bag and closed the door, making out her silhouette easily since his eyes were acclimated to the darkness. He couldn't see her features but she had all her limbs and hadn't been crying.

"Is that how you greet all your guests here?" he asked in a light voice.

She snorted. "I heard you coming and I wasn't expecting anyone."

"So you were going to shoot them and leave them rotting in the swamp." It wasn't a question but a testament that he knew what she was capable of if it came down to her life or someone else's.

"Glad you have faith in me."

"I do. Baby, are you okay?" He took a step forward, afraid to reach for her but unable to stop himself. His hands met cool, bare flesh and he realized his sight hadn't picked out the fact she wore only a sports bra and panties.

A growl left him as he hauled her close and buried his face in her hair. "God, you feel so right," he said before he could choke it off.

She went still in his hold, not putting her arms around him or responding in any way. "Hawk, we need to talk."

He let her go and stooped to unzip his duffel. "I brought the Christmas cheer." He went to the kitchen and after fumbling in a drawer, found a corkscrew. He turned to look at Tyler. "Mind if I light a second candle?"

"You can just turn on the light."

"I like it this way."

"Why, are you hiding something?" Suspicion rang in her voice.

"Besides a few cuts and bruises from that last mission, nothing at all. But you look lovely in the candlelight. And… it's easier for me to talk to you in the dark." He uncorked the good wine that had cost him a fortune and he hadn't batted an eye at paying for. When he handed her a glass, he said, "Swirl it. Let it breathe a bit first."

She wrapped her fingers around the stem and sank to the sofa. He sat next to her and swirled the contents of his glass, inhaling the rich scents and considering his words.

"Why is it easier to talk to me in the dark?"

He took a sip. Swallowed. Set down his glass on a side table. "Tyler, that last mission… It fucked me up a bit and I'm not ashamed to admit it. I need to talk to someone. Will you listen?"

"Oh Hawk… of course." She sipped her wine and drew her legs up so she could angle her body toward his. The candlelight beaded along her smooth thighs and did things to his insides, but he hadn't been lying about what he'd said — he needed her.

The fucked up story came out smooth at first and where shit had gone south, his storytelling did too. It came out in a series of speed bumps that ended with him leaning forward with his elbows on his knees, head in his hands.

The sofa cushion shifted under him as she moved closer. She set down her wine and rested a hand on his back.

"It all sounds like something out of a horror movie," he grated out. "I hope I don't give you nightmares."

"I'm made of tougher stuff than that."

Now that the tale was out, a pressure lifted off his shoulders. He drew a full breath and caught the fragrant notes of her bodywash. An awareness settled over him.

He straightened and reached for his wine though his urge was to tug her across his thighs, bend her over his arm and kiss her.

She really was lovely in the candlelight, all gleaming curves. He tried not to snap off the stem of the glass he held.

Raising her glass, she said, "To the buried past."

He wasn't so sure he liked that toast, but when it came to the ghosts he'd just released from his soul, then it worked for him. "To the buried past."

They drank.

He poured them more. By the third glass, the strong wine was beginning to creep over him, and he felt that telltale relaxing of muscles that told him he'd better guard his lips too. The surefire way to drive Tyler away from him was to tell her how he felt about her.

She leaned back against the sofa, legs still curled to the side. What he wouldn't give to glide his hand between the warm seam of her thighs, up to that treasure.

"Do you feel better after talking over what happened?" she asked, her words quiet.

"Yes, I do. Thank you."

She lowered her wine glass and looked at him over the brim. In the candlelight, her irises appeared black. "Funny how just telling the details sometimes makes them all... fly away." She fluttered her fingers in the air.

He cocked his head. "Tyler?"

She met his stare.

"Are you drunk?"

She shook her head and then said, "Maybe just a little fuggy. Fuzzy. Foggy." She giggled.

He took the glass from her hands. She let him, eyes glowing and her breaths came faster.

He gave in to his desires and finally tugged her across his lap. Her backside hit his groin and he released a groan of need. The half hard-on he'd been battling for the past half hour hit full-blown erection.

She slid her arms around his neck and tilted her face up. An invitation to kiss her? He was damn well taking it as one.

He swept her mouth with his tongue, gaining all the heady flavors of wine she'd consumed, along with a faint trace of mint as if she'd already brushed her teeth for bed. Good — she was ready to hit the sheets.

Drawing her thigh around him so she was straddling his waist, he stood with her. The wine glass wasn't settled far enough on the edge of the coffee table and it hit the floor.

"I'll clean it tomorrow," he muttered against her lips.

She clung to his shoulders. "You better. My *maman* won't be happy if it stains."

"I'll find some salt."

She giggled. When he burst into the room they'd shared the time before, she grasped him by the nape and yanked him down for another kiss. Dizzy with pleasure and powerful emotions whipping through his system, he stood in the middle of the room, kissing her back.

Letting the moment fill him up and overflow.

God, he was in love with her. But the moment he spoke the words, she'd turn ice-cold in his arms and walk away. He knew Tyler.

Best to caress and ease into things. To convince her that she wasn't only falling into his arms because one or both needed comfort. If he had to spend every day till New Year's convincing her with orgasm after orgasm, well, somebody had to take one for the team.

He broke the kiss long enough to get them to the bed. The covers were already turned down. Had she been cuddled up here when she'd heard him approach the dock?

"I still owe you for pointing that gun in my face." He nipped at her earlobe, and she cried out.

154

"You're pointing your gun at me right now." She rocked her hips so her pussy brushed against his steely cock.

"Naughty girl. Santa's gonna bring you a whole sack of toys."

"This game's getting creepy."

He chuckled and buried his face between her breasts, nuzzling till he reached her hard nipple and took it into his mouth through the cloth of her bra.

He raised his head abruptly. "No good. I want you bare."

As he removed her bra and panties along with his own shirt and boots, he drank in every long, heated look she gave him, committing them all to the vault of his mind. He'd never felt this way about a woman before, and he wasn't about to give up. But if she demanded they end it, at least he'd have his memories.

Pushing the idea from his mind, he took up where he left off. Her nipples.

They were so distended and swollen, and he couldn't suck them enough for her liking. She kept moving his head from one to the other, until he sucked one and pinched the other before switching.

She ran her hands over his chest and down to his cock. "I want to suck you, Bo."

How could any man deny that request?

An uneven breath left him and he gave a jerky nod.

He rolled onto his back to allow her to lean over him, soft hair brushing over his naked chest as she worked at his fly. Then he lifted his hips so she could push his pants and briefs down his thighs.

She moaned at the sight of his hard cock. And he moaned at the sight of her taking him in her mouth.

Inch by inch she swallowed him until the distended head hit the back of her throat.

He threaded his fingers through her hair and held her there, mesmerized by the enveloping warmth of her lips and one hell of a view.

His abs dipped as she pulled back on his cock and then laved her tongue around the tip.

"Jesus Christ."

"I thought I was Mrs. Claus."

"Dirty girl. Take it all."

"Yes, sir." She flashed her eyes at him as she sucked him right to the root. The soft pull of her mouth, dragging at his flesh, drawing his orgasm up from his balls—

He threw his head back. The wine was working in his favor. He wasn't going to come—not yet and sure as hell not prematurely. He planned to finger her until she screamed for more and then he'd lick her clean. Only then would he slam his cock inside that tight pussy of hers and unload every ounce of cum that'd been building up for her for weeks.

Steeling his muscles, he bit back the grunts of need as she sucked and worked him with her tongue like it was her full-time job. If he had his way, he'd keep her there forever. But the way she stroked under his balls was quickly stripping away all of his alcohol-induced self-control.

He wrapped her hair around his fist and drew her head up. She released him with a pop, lips wet and swollen from sucking him.

"You're going to make me come just from looking at you, baby. Get up here and sit on my face."

* * * * *

Tyler's head wasn't so fuzzy that she couldn't recognize it wasn't the wine talking. This was straight up, no-holds-barred desire. Somehow this man had jumped in to rescue her and had ended up ripping the rug out from under her with his demands for her to open up to him in all ways.

Besides, Hawk was damn good in bed.

He knew his way around a fitting room too.

Her thighs squeezed around his ears as he lapped at her clit. The bundle of nerves shot off sparks of electric lust, and she tossed her head back on a moan. With each rotation of his tongue, she was climbing higher and higher, so close to falling off the proverbial ledge that no ropes could hold her back now.

She let go of all her past history with Hawk and accepted him as the man she knew now. Not the man who was friends with her brothers, riding the outer edges of their family unit but someone she was grabbing by the shirt and dragging into the center of her world.

Crazy but true. Or the wine might be talking now, who knew?

She wiggled back and forth on his tongue, and his groan vibrated her. The fact that he loved making sure she felt good and was cared for far exceeded her knowledge of men. Everybody she'd slept with was interested in his own pleasure and just gave the hasty rubs and tugs that passed for foreplay.

Bo wasn't like that. He took his time, licking her slit up and down until she started to tremble. Then gliding a fingertip into her pussy, just enough to tease yet send her rocketing through the sky.

She gasped and rode his lips and tongue as her pulsations claimed her sanity. A cry that couldn't possibly have come from her actually did come from her. He planted his hands firmly on her hips and helped her rise and fall again and again until a final rasp left her and she fell forward.

She held onto the wall to keep from toppling off.

He took care of that for her, lifting her off his face like the muscle man he was and laying her out on the mattress. She looked up at him as he shimmied off the rest of his clothes.

With cock in hand, he nudged her thighs apart with his knee and sank balls-deep.

She spread her legs wide to take him a fraction deeper, and they shared a groan of delight.

Bo cupped her face and looked into her eyes. "I love the feeling of you pulling me inside you."

His words gave her a thrill low in her belly. "I love the feeling of you stretching me."

"Seems like we're pretty good at this game." He gave her a crooked grin that melted her insides and — she was more hesitant to admit — her heart.

He lifted her with a hand beneath her ass, drawing her up and into his every plunge. And she was slowly shaking apart. She dug her heel into his backside, yanking him wildly into her. The old mattress springs screamed in protest, just adding to the music of their passionate lovemaking.

When she slid a hand around his nape and pulled him down for a tongue-tangling kiss, his long moan of release sounded a split second before the first hot splash of cum hit her insides.

She cried out as her own orgasm hit. He fucked her faster and harder until her body unwound and loosened around his length.

She let her heel slip down his thigh and fall to the bed.

Gently, he lowered her, pressing kisses over her forehead and eyes, her cheek and jaw until he finally claimed her mouth. The kiss was long and deep, heralding far more than she was prepared to accept, admit or claim.

Maybe it was the twinkle lights, she thought. The wine and the twinkle lights.

Whatever magic was at work in her life right now, she'd come home after a bad situation and found something she'd never expected. Not only a man who knew her, trusted her and could pleasure her absolutely... but one who was her friend.

* * * * *

"That's it, baby. Ride my fingers. Feel my pushing up into you. Your pussy's getting so tight." He bit off the words, and her body responded full force with an orgasm that had her bucking and calling out his name.

The fifth orgasm was no less amazing than the rest, and if anything she was getting more wound up.

He eased his fingers from her pussy and smeared the juices over her sensitive clit. She jumped and turned onto her side, staring at him through a fog of sleep and the wine they'd just about finished off.

He reached for the bottle on the nightstand and took a swig. When he lowered it, he smacked his lips. "Oops. I finished it off."

She chuckled and took the bottle.

"It's empty, baby," he said with some regret.

She gave him a devilish cock of her brow. "I like to reuse." She drew the mouth of the bottle between her thighs.

"God, woman. You're so damn sexy and I love your dirty mind." He watched her slip the neck into her pussy and give it a few hip thrusts. She eased it in and out, and he looked on, gaze intense.

Something about how he loved watching her get off had her locked and loaded and ready to blow over and over again.

He reached down and drew the bottle free of her folds. Then he licked off the rim, tipping it back to swallow the last drop clinging to the glass.

He groaned and sank over her, filling her with his cock just the way she wanted him to. With her legs wrapped around him and his dark stare penetrating hers, she couldn't think of anyplace she'd rather be.

"You've drained me, baby. I'll be shooting blanks. But I can't... seem... to stop." He punctuated his words with hip thrusts.

"You need the target practice," she whispered, dragging her teeth over his shoulder. He hummed out how much he liked that and twisted his mouth into hers. Claiming her all over again.

After another shared release, they collapsed in each other's arms.

He drew his fingers up and down her spine, and she loved that his touch wasn't wimpy or ticklish but just right.

"So how was the party?" His chest rumbled under her ear.

"I left before it started."

"You did?"

"Yes, I..." She stopped, unsure how he'd take what she'd been about to say.

"Tyler, I think we're past all that holding back bullshit, aren't we?"

She drew in a deep breath and let it out slowly. "I found out that you'd been called away and I left the party."

He tensed, and she couldn't gauge anything without seeing his expression. When she moved her head on his shoulder to see his face, she found him wearing a shit-eating grin.

She thumped him with her fist. "I can see that satisfies you."

"Damn straight."

"I don't know if I could have been in the same room with you after the fitting room thing."

His grin widened, and her heart skipped a beat. He was so gorgeous and she was content to stay with him in bed till next year.

If they did, though, her brothers would send out a search party and find them naked and entwined.

"The fitting room was fucking hot, baby."

A small shiver ran over her skin. "It was."

He folded her more tightly in his arms. "Maybe we can go in the closet and recreate it." He shot a look toward the side of the room where the closet was located.

She laughed. "It's stuffed with rafts and beach towels. We'd never fit."

"Oh we fit." His growled words fell across her lips, and he kissed her.

Dammit, her mind wouldn't shut off right now and just give in to her body's desires. Soon her leave would be up and her immediate orders were to return to base following New Year's. It was down to days now and time was disappearing fast. She had to end things with Bo.

Or decide on a new path for her life.

He brushed his lips across hers one more time before looking deep into her eyes and smiling. He slapped her hip, making her jump. "Into the shower with you, temptress."

"Then what?"

He arched a brow. "Breakfast. I'm starved. I hope you can cook an acceptable egg."

"Depends on what you call acceptable. Why don't you cook it?"

"All right, I will. I don't mind taking care of my woman. Sausage or bacon rations in the fridge?"

"Both in the freezer. You'll have to thaw them out."

"Bacon then. Takes less time." He pinched her ass and she squealed, leaping out of bed. He gave her an appreciative look as she sashayed to the bathroom, swinging her hips enticingly.

At the door, she tossed him a coy glance. "See ya in ten."

As soon as she got into the shower and replayed all the events on the past night, she had no idea how to piece together answers. She and Bo might be fooling themselves and splitting was the best course of action in the long run. He had his life, she had hers.

It sure was sweeter together these past few weeks, though.

She sighed and lathered her hair, letting her mind wander. Too many times it rounded back to being here at the cabin with her family—and Bo at her side, as her lover, her friend, her everything.

Rinsing her hair, she murmured, "Happy holidays to me. Santa's brought a big, fat dilemma."

Chapter Ten

Out here in the middle of nowhere, the only phone that worked was a satellite phone, and Hawk carried one with him. But right at this moment, with the sound of the shower running and bacon sizzling on the stovetop, the last thing he wanted to hear was it ring.

"Hawkeye," he answered in a rough voice.

"This is Lieutenant Colonel Darren. Colonel Jackson requests you in his office in an hour."

Jesus.

"I can't make it in an hour."

"An hour and a half then. And I have it in my knowledge that Tyler Knight is with you."

Fuck. What the hell was going on?

"Why do you need Ms. Knight?"

"The colonel wants to see her too."

"What's this about?" Hawkeye asked, casting a look at the bedroom door and praying Tyler didn't step out until he knew exactly what was taking place and why they were both in on it.

"You know the rules, Hawk." Darren let down his guard for a moment. "Just get your ass in here and bring Knight."

Shit.

"We'll be there."

He stared blankly at the pan of sizzling bacon for a moment. Talk about bad timing. Just as he was breaking through Tyler's tough exterior and getting her to open up to him—and dare he say the possibility of a relationship?—this shit happened. Would it always be this way? Making plans and breaking them for a mission?

Except this time Jackson wanted both of them in his office, and he couldn't imagine why. It wasn't against the rules for either Tyler as a Marine or him as an OFFSUS agent to date each other.

He heard the shower shut off and turned the bacon calmly with a fork. Inside, he was far from calm, though. They had to appear before Jackson but he wasn't about to risk the bond he'd formed with Tyler, either.

Weighing his options came to no good decision, always ending in being court martialed. Finally, he turned off the burner and placed the bacon on a plate covered in paper towel. The scrambled eggs he'd already made remained warm under lid, and he'd been starving a moment ago but now had no appetite.

As soon as he told Tyler what was going down, she would refuse to eat too.

He had to tell her right now if they were to make it to Jackson's on time.

He walked into the bedroom and found her naked.

He scrubbed a hand over his face to try to cut the shock of seeing her beautiful, nude body feet away, enticing him with perky nipples and that round ass he wanted to claim as his own in time.

Maybe on our honeymoon.

Damn, he was in deep, always had been when it came to this woman.

She turned and caught sight of him. "Are you just going to stand there staring at me, pervert?"

He pushed out a breath that held a bit of amusement at her insult. God, she was so lovely and all he wanted was to drag her back into bed with him and keep her there all week. But it wasn't to be.

"Baby, I got a phone call."

She went still, hands raised to button her top. "I didn't hear it."

"You were in the shower."

"You have a mission?" She dropped her gaze to her buttons and began working them quickly, her nimble fingers moving up the row until her bare skin was all tucked out of sight.

He couldn't stop himself from touching her and moved up behind her. Wrapping his arms around her, drawing her back against his chest. He kissed the side of her throat and then rested his head on her shoulder. "Jackson wants both of us."

She yanked out of his hold and spun on him. "For what?"

"Your guess is as good as mine, but they expect us in about an hour and twenty minutes, so we need to paddle our asses out of here with all haste."

"Shit." She spat the cuss and began jerking on her jeans and a pair of boots. She slanted a look at him. "You think they have a problem with us being together?"

"I don't know how they could."

"If Jackson knows, so do my brothers."

He dragged in a breath. "I'm prepared to face that." All at once, he had to make her know everything. He walked up to her and grabbed her hands, enfolding her fingers tight in his grasp. "Tyler..."

She searched his gaze. "Oh God, Hawk, don't do this right now."

"I have to. Now shut up."

Her jaw dropped and he grinned as he used a forefinger to gently close her jaw. Looking into her eyes, he said, "You have me completely fucking mesmerized, you know that, Knight?"

"I—" She broke off. "Mesmerized?"

"You have no idea. I can't stop thinking about you. I play out conversations I want to have with you when I'm sitting in the middle of a swamp with bullets zinging by my head."

She fidgeted but he held her hands prisoner. Just as he opened his mouth to tell her exactly how important she was in his life and how deep she'd dug her hooks into his heart, the SAT phone rang again.

As if she'd been waiting for an excuse to escape him, Tyler lunged for the phone in his pocket. She snatched it out and brought it to her ear.

"Hawk, you'd better fucking present yourself to me and my four brothers right after you stand before Jackson." Her brother Ben's voice came over loud and clear.

Her face drained of color and she darted her tongue over her dry lower lip. "Ben?"

"Jesus, it's true. Goddammit, Tyler, what are you doing with Hawk? I didn't want to believe it."

"Uh... Here's Hawk." Her wide eyes said it all as she shoved the phone at him.

He took it from her and held her gaze as he spoke. "Yeah, she's with me."

"For how fucking long have you been fucking our sister right under our noses?"

Tyler winced as her brother reverted to his love of the F word.

Hawk looked right into her eyes when he said, "Since Kandahar."

"Fucking hell," Ben bit off.

169

Tyler let out a girly growl of anger.

"You're facing me — all of us Knights — as soon as you get her home."

"She's not coming home."

"What?" Ben's voice was deadly calm.

"Jackson wants her too. Don't worry — she's in good hands."

At that, Tyler started to slap at his shoulders and biceps. Hawk would have laughed if it didn't actually sting and she didn't look about to drown him off the dock in the bayou. He fought off her anger by finally throwing her on the bed and pinning her down. Her eyes shot bullets at him, each little fleck in her eyes fiercer than the next.

"Dammit, I'm calling Jackson right now. Why the hell does he want Tyler?" Ben demanded.

"Hey!" She heard her brother's words and snatched the phone from Hawk. "Why the hell wouldn't he want *me*? You aren't the only Knights who are sought out for your skill."

"Tyler, I'm going to have a long talk with you too. I can't believe you were hiding this thing with Hawk from us."

With true amusement, Hawk watched her open her mouth in an attempt to speak, shut it again and then hit a button on the phone to end the call.

Taking the phone from her hand, he set it aside and swooped in to claim her lips. She struggled for half a heartbeat before giving in to him and slipping her arms around his neck.

It didn't take two sweeps of his tongue to realize he couldn't go on without taking it right to the end of the line. Tyler did that to a man.

He pushed back on his elbows and stared into her eyes. "They won't be angry after I explain everything."

"Oh no. You're not doing the explaining. I'll do it."

"Not without me there."

"Like hell."

"Why not?" He nibbled along her delicate jaw, and she tipped her head back to give him access.

"Because you're likely to tell them things that aren't true."

"Such as?"

"Such as it's more than just sex."

He locked her in his gaze. "It is more than sex."

"To you maybe, which is the trouble. Hawk, we can't—"

"Be late to see Jackson. Get up and grab your stuff. Meet me in the canoe."

Without another word, he did a pushup off the mattress, picked up his phone and his bag and walked out, leaving her speechless and probably as pissed off as a gator on a fishhook.

And not kissed nearly enough.

* * * * *

Just great. Her brothers were on the warpath, ready to string up Hawk and leave him for dead for fucking around with her. She should have avoided all this drama by resisting the man in the first place.

As if I could.

He drew her in like fire to an arsonist, and each time he got near her, she felt like she was burning up.

She continued to shoot him looks out of the corner of her eye as he rowed them out of the bayou and then put her in his jeep and drove her back to New Orleans.

"I'm not presentable enough for Jackson." At least she'd showered and didn't still smell like sex and man.

Hawk threw her a glance. "You're beautiful."

"Jackson doesn't want beautiful. He wants the Marine."

He looked her over more carefully, taking his eyes off the road as he rolled through the gates of base. "That's what I'm afraid of," he mumbled.

With no response to that, she remained silent. She didn't even know if she should be offended that Hawk was stifling the Marine side of her — if he was. She had no idea what he meant right now, and she was too nervous about meeting the colonel to think on it more.

172

When they walked in, she pushed her way in front of Hawk. But he eased around her and refused to let her past.

"Get out of my way."

"I didn't take you for one of those people who has to always be first. Being the sixth child and all." His words dropped like moonshine syrup over her *maman's* fresh homemade waffles, which she could go for right about now.

She was still full of bacon, though. Before leaving, she'd dropped it all into a bag and she and Hawk had shared a picnic of sorts as he rowed them back to the vehicle. Looking back, she realized eating bacon while rowing through the bayou might have been romantic under other circumstances.

Reaching out, she tried to shove Hawk out of the way so she could enter Jackson's office first and look like she was the Marine who was raring to go. But he refused to let her by, blocking her as if to... protect her?

She narrowed her eyes at his broad back but couldn't see inside his skull. Which was probably a good thing—it had to be thick with dirty things she could see running behind his eyes when he looked at her but he never said.

As they approached the door, one of the guards opened it for them. Hawk entered before her, but she moved up next to him and stood at attention before Colonel Jackson.

"Well, aren't you two the pair?" Jackson mused.

Her stomach slithered with worry. The last thing she wanted in her vocation was to appear to have girlish desires. She had to be strong and immune to everything but doing her job and doing it well.

"At ease. You're a minute late."

That minute had been spent with Hawk pinning her to the bed back in the cabin. She couldn't bring herself to regret it though.

"Traffic, sir." Hawk spent a lot of time getting orders from Jackson, so he stood in a relaxed pose. But she felt like biting off all her nails. She didn't even want to think of what her brothers had done over the years to piss off this man.

She stood waiting for the reason they'd been brought here. She tried not to look around his stark office. This hard man was also her brother Ben's father-in-law, and while he clearly was warmer in his personal life, throwing barbecues and inviting the whole Knight Ops team, Jackson didn't have so much as a picture of his baby granddaughter on his desk.

Not for the first time, she realized how odd it was that they all must compartmentalize their working life and personal life so the edges never brushed each other.

Jackson eyed her, and she went still, staring at the buttons of his uniform. She'd seen him when Ben and Dahlia married, of course, but he'd intimidated her even then.

174

Abruptly, he turned to Hawk. "There's an issue that needs your attention in Kandahar, Hawkeye."

"On it, sir."

Jackson flicked his gaze to her. "And she's going with you."

"No." It didn't come out as anything but rude, and she stifled a gasp.

Jackson's exterior was calm as he got in Hawk's face. They glared at each other, and she wondered how Hawk had the balls to stand up to the colonel this way.

"Did you have something to say, Hawkeye?"

"She isn't going, sir."

"She damn well is. Meet your new civil affairs specialist."

She jolted but tried not to show it.

Jackson pivoted to her. "You've struck a rapport with the authorities there, and there's a situation where we could use your skills."

"No," Hawk said in a louder voice.

She turned to him. "Stop."

He met her gaze, and she saw at last that yes, he was trying to protect her. And no wonder after what had happened to her in Kandahar last time, but this would be different.

It was her job to go.

Silent, Jackson observed them.

"I should have you stood against a wall and shot for insubordination, Hawkeye. But America needs you too much, so I will just have you stand down now while I speak to Knight here."

She could hear his teeth grinding from several feet away, but Hawk said nothing more.

She looked to Jackson, her stomach a nervous pit of butterflies. "Sir?"

"OFFSUS just stopped a small ship coming from international waters full of refugees."

Her gaze lifted to his and she held her breath.

"They're all children. Two hundred and six of them, taken by land to the Arabian Sea."

She let her breath trickle out, feeling her heart going out to that many children separated from their parents. Shipped away for what reason? To provide them with a chance at a better life?

"Where are the parents, sir?" Hawk asked from beside her.

Jackson pivoted his head to look at him, his steely gray brow arched. "That information is not known, but what we do know is there are over two hundred children in need of shelter and aid at Kandahar Air Base. We need your skills to speak with them, Knight, to get them to talk and give us the names of their parents who sent them away."

She couldn't help but ask. "But what happens when we find them?"

"The parents will be questioned to see if they're fit. It's a form of cruelty to send them to a new country without more than a few provisions and no adults to see them safe other than a shady ship captain."

She nodded. It was terrible and yet, they must have reasons they were deeply passionate about to take such risks with their offspring.

"I'll go, sir."

"In the next hour, Knight."

She nodded.

"Now both of you get out of your civilian clothes. Transport is at thirteen-thirty."

They snapped their salutes and were dismissed. As they walked past the guard, she glared at Hawk.

"Don't give me that look."

"I don't need your protection, Hawk."

His dark eyes burned with some emotion she might count as anger if she hadn't seen that same look in bed with him. "You don't need it, but I want to offer it. Okay, Civil Affairs Specialist Knight?"

Their strides matched as they headed away from Jackson's office.

"But why are we suddenly linked?" she asked.

"Maybe he thinks we make a good team. Maybe having a man and woman working with two hundred children who are basically orphaned will help keep them calm and provide a nurturing front. Mom and pops."

"God. Over two hundred. Can you imagine coming across that vessel?"

"Yes, unfortunately, I can. I've seen a lot of things." He stopped and hovered near. "Are you sure you're all right with this, Tyler? That your emotions won't get the better of you?"

She couldn't believe he was throwing her behavior after her last visit to Kandahar in her face.

She narrowed her eyes and said, "Go to hell, Hawk." She strode away and rounded a corner, but his chuckle followed her.

"That's my girl."

Chapter Eleven

Hawk had spent the ten minutes it took to outfit himself in uniform and gear trying to think of a way to keep Tyler out of this godforsaken mess. Nothing good could come out of her going back to Afghanistan.

He considered bringing a member of the Knight Ops team in her place, but they all had wives and if they could manage to evade a mission and spend Christmas with their families, they should. Hawk had no family and didn't care about eggnog or presents or Yule logs.

He did, however, care a fucking lot about Tyler.

He grinned at her telling him to go to hell. Her spunk got him every damn time.

A few minutes later he stood outside, pacing in front of the transport waiting for her. When she emerged from the building he gave her an approving once-over.

She glared at him harder as she neared.

"Fashionably late but worth it," he commented.

She looked ready to wring his neck. He hoped she did it with those strong thighs of hers so he could still access her pussy with his tongue.

He pitched his voice low. "I have to admit I prefer the lingerie from the dressing room but you do fill out a uniform to perfection."

Staring straight ahead, she walked by him and climbed into the waiting SUV that would take them to the government jet.

Hawk hung back a second to appreciate the curves of her ass in those cargo pants before catching up. The minute he slammed the door and reached for his seatbelt, she rounded on him.

"Stop treating me like your girlfriend, Hawk."

He shot a glance at the driver who was trying his best to ignore their spat.

Hawk drew in a deep breath and let it out slowly, counting to twenty for patience. "You know for somebody so smart, you're sure as hell dense at times. What the hell do you think you are to me?"

She sliced a look at the driver and whispered, "A bed partner?"

"You think you're just a lay to me? Christ, woman, I thought you knew me better."

"You can't tell me I'm the only woman you've been with."

"Well in my thirty years, no, you're not. But since having you that first time, yeah. And it's true I never saw what was right under my nose. You were a kid when we met."

She let out a low growl of warning, which he ignored.

"But," he went on, "I have gotten to see a new side of you, Tyler. The woman sitting here right now is strong, capable, independent and sexy as hell, and what you need is a man who loves those things about you. Who doesn't want to change you."

"So by telling Jackson I wasn't going on this mission is how you do that? Explain that to me, Hawk." Her hair was pinned back in a low bun that on some women would look severe, but it only served to highlight her feminine features.

Hell. He was going to have to tell her.

"I fucked up back there."

She gaped at him.

"I shouldn't have stepped in but it was my gut instinct to keep you here instead of going."

"Why?"

"Because you're not the only person conflicted between your duty and personal life. You think I wake up each morning like this?" He waved a hand over his attire and all the gear he carried to handle any situation thrown in his path. "Under these clothes I'm just a man, Tyler. And that man is in love."

She straightened, staring at him.

"With you," he clarified.

Her eyelids closed, and for a moment he didn't know if she was affected by his admission or shutting down on him.

He reached for her hand and she didn't fight him. Leaning close, he whispered, "I love you, Tyler.

181

Forgive me for trying to shield you, but it's in my nature."

After a moment of silence, she opened her eyes and said, "I can handle it."

Her words struck him like blows.

No I-love-you back.

No acknowledgement of his admission whatsoever.

He let go of her hand and sat back, staring at his hands and then turning his attention to the landscape flying by the window. He was man enough to lay his heart on the line, and she had nothing to say at all.

It figured that his Miss Right turned out to be a stubborn-ass Knight.

* * * * *

When Tyler walked into the huge room holding all the children they'd stopped from leaving Afghanistan, she halted in her tracks.

This was the day of hard truths for her. *First Bo tells me he loves me and I realize I love him back.*

Then she found herself standing before over two hundred kids, realizing they were about to arrive on American soil to make their own way or become victims of a human trafficking trade or worse.

And that she had to do something about both.

She felt Hawk's body heat on her back. "Jesus Christ," he muttered.

She nodded.

"First order is find the man in charge and see what's going on."

Galvanized into action, she picked out the uniformed officer standing at the head of the room and strode toward him.

The room was far too silent to be housing children. Hell, she and her brothers and sister had made more noise than this in their living room. The kids were terrified, and that was the thing she had to fix straight away.

"Major Slate." Hawk said with a salute.

She followed. "Major."

"At ease. It's me who should be saluting you both. This is one fuck of a mess, isn't it?" The man was in his late forties with graying hair and a hard look about his features. When he scanned the room at large, his eyes burned with an intensity that told Tyler he might have children of his own and be thinking of all the unimaginable things that might have happened to these kids if they'd reached their destination.

She met the major's gaze. "What needs to be done, sir?"

"They've had food and been giving pillows and blankets, but many are bad off without proper clothing or shoes."

"I have some ideas about how to get those."

Hawk swung his stare to her, and she felt a slithering of desire coupled with a leap of her heart at the memory of his words. He was in love with her.

The major continued, "We've got some translators trying to pull information from the kids, but most won't speak at all."

"They were told not to," Hawk said.

She agreed. "Have we found any of the parents? Have any stepped forward to claim their children?"

"Not a one. They put them on a fucking vessel that was barely seaworthy. It was like setting sail on a fucking raft with a single captain who might as well have been running a 2-stroke."

Being born to the bayou, she knew the major was belittling the situation even further with reference to such a small boat engine. Frustration buried lines in his forehead as he looked over the group again.

"I'll look into the clothing situation first and then start speaking to them." Her only thought was to reunite them with their families, where they belonged. The city was sometimes a frightening place, and the people had been desperate. But the children were still better off — safer — with their relatives.

"Hawkeye, I've got something to show you." The major took him off, and Hawk threw her a look.

She gave a nod that she'd be all right.

Having spent time in Kandahar, she knew some of the merchants and had an idea of just where to go for aid. She found a private who was eager to be her assistant, and she made some phone calls. After securing as many items of clothing and shoes as she could, she sent a couple privates on the errand to collect them.

Then she took up a notepad and pen and slowly approached a group of the children. They stared at her with wide eyes full of fear. Her heartstrings yanked. Dammit, they should be home with their loved ones.

These children did not celebrate Christmas the way American ones did, but surely there was something more cheerful awaiting them than a long, terrifying journey by boat in overcrowded conditions.

She had to find their families.

Squatting, she waved at one child to come nearer. He paused for a moment with uncertainty and then grabbed the hand of a little girl next to him. Towing her along, he came closer to Tyler.

She put a smile on her face for them both. First, she gave a customary greeting of hand over her heart and a slight nod. In their language, she told them her name.

They stared at her.

Pointing at the girl, she asked her name.

Silence.

She tried the boy and got sealed lips as well.

Okay, so this wouldn't be that easy. She spoke to them for a few minutes in a calming voice, just telling them what was happening and she understood they must be scared. That got a slight nod from the girl but the boy who must be no more than six, remained stiffly at her side.

"And this must be your sister," she said in his language.

His big dark eyes shifted with something like pride, and Tyler could only imagine the weight that had been placed on this young boy's shoulders to get them safely to a new land.

She spread out a blanket and invited them to sit on it while she worked with a few other children. After a half hour, she realized she wasn't going to get anywhere with these kids.

As a teen, she'd done her share of babysitting jobs, and one thing that had always worked to break the ice was food.

She told the five kids circled on the blanket around her that she'd return in a minute. Then she crossed the room to some air force personnel.

"I need candy."

One chuckled. "Come again?"

"I know you've got to have some American chocolate on this base, and I need crates of it. Also, fruit or pastries."

The officers exchanged a look and then went to do her bidding. She scanned the wide room and her heart ached. What if she wasn't able to help any of these children?

She didn't see Hawk either, and she didn't know if that was for the better or worse. She needed time to think on her emotions. Far from impulsive, she wasn't about to just jump at his admission of love and start a relationship.

Except, hadn't they already started?

"Knight."

She turned at her name. Her eyes flew open and a grin spread across her face as the two privates she'd sent into the village returned carrying big black garbage bags stuffed full.

She hurried forward. "Clothes and shoes?"

"Yes. More in the truck being unloaded right now."

"Put it all along that wall." She pointed, and they moved off with nods.

At that moment, she turned and saw a flash of red. When one of the guys she'd asked for the sweet treats came back bearing a big bag. All the children's eyes were glued to him. A murmur ran through the group.

She grinned at the officer. "Thank you. I think this might act as an ice breaker."

He handed her the bag with a small bow. "Michaels is rounding up more."

"Great! Meet me in the middle of the room and bring a camera."

"What's the camera for?" he asked.

"It's get-your-photo-taken-with-Mrs.-Claus. Though they don't know what that is. But we can label each with the names they provide to me."

As soon as she approached the kids on the blanket where she'd left them, some of the earlier trepidation fled and the girl even cracked a smile for her.

Inspired, Tyler sat cross-legged on the blanket. After handing out some candy, she had all five kids smiling and managed to hedge their names from them as well as those of their parents. And the frightened little girl was in her lap.

* * * * *

When Hawk entered the room again and saw the kids clustering around something in the center of the room, he knew immediately that it was Tyler. He let out a laugh.

Leave it to Tyler to find a way to bribe over two hundred kids. As he moved closer, he saw she sat on a chair with bags around her and the private at her side was busy snapping photos while another wrote down names and Tyler handed out presents, which was clothing, shoes and it looked like all the sugar foods she could find.

Hawk swallowed the lump rising in his throat. How she'd managed to bring a spot of kindness to the situation was anyone's guess. Then again, he'd always known she was smart and resourceful as well as strikingly gorgeous.

Her cheeks were flushed pink with happiness, and her smile never quit. When the next in line was a very shy child, she coaxed and cajoled until he inched near her. Hawk couldn't blame the kid—Tyler was like a beautiful butterfly everyone wanted to look at closer.

The kid stood in front of her, unsmiling. She said something to him and then plucked the uniform hat off her head. Candy rained down and the kids cracked up laughing. The little boy giggled too, and he lunged forward to gather up the treats.

His photo was snapped and he spoke his name in a quiet voice as well as his father's. Then the next child came forward.

As if feeling Hawk's gaze on her, Tyler looked up. Their gazes locked, and the happiness in her eyes seemed to swell in magnitude as she stared at him. With a crook of her finger, she beckoned him to come to her.

He slowly moved through the group of pipsqueaks until he reached her side. "This is amazing," he said.

She nodded. "I think I see how Christmas works now. Want to play Santa's helper for a while?"

"Damn, that sounds dirty," he murmured close to her ear.

A shiver rolled through her, and she bit down on her lower lip. "Later, Bo. Just hand out the clothes for now."

"How do I know what size is best?"

"We're just guessing. The bag on your right is bigger children's sizes and on the left are smaller."

Heart full of wonder and love, he knelt on the hard floor to assist in the merriest of ways he could think of with the woman he loved at his side.

After the final little one received her presents, she plunked down very close to Hawk to unwrap her candy. Tyler laughed and had the officer snap a photo of them.

"Now one of our merry Mr. and Mrs. Claus," the officer said, camera poised.

Hawk's heart pulsed faster. Did everyone see the love on his face right now? They had to see how Hawk felt about this woman.

When she leaned close and a photograph taken, he took the chance to whisper, "Wait till I get you alone. I'll show you what a good girl you've been."

Reaching down, she found his fingers and squeezed. The action put more hope in his heart than he wanted to admit. Maybe she hadn't been immune to his admission of love as he'd believed but just needed time to process it. Knowing Tyler, she was holding a grudge over wanting to tell him she loved him first.

If she did.

God, he hoped she did. He couldn't imagine life without her or going back to being just acquaintances, seeing each other in passing and making small talk at the Knights' gatherings.

Dammit, he wanted it all. And Christmas miracles wouldn't just happen for this group of children. Hawk had a plan.

Chapter Twelve

As Hawk opened the door of the Humvee for Tyler, she stared at him. "How did you get access to this?"

"I have my ways. Pulled about a hundred strings with Jackson. I might even owe him my firstborn son. Get in."

She did, exhausted from travel, jetlag and a very satisfying day. The children were tucked in to their makeshift beds on the floor and she could rest a bit easier as the government did their best to locate the parents who had sent their children away.

She sank into the leather seat and Hawk shut the door. A second later he climbed behind the wheel and started the engine.

"Where are we going? Aren't we going to get in trouble for leaving?" she asked as he made it to the road and turned.

He shot her a look. "I told you I fixed it with Jackson. Christmas is about surprises. You'll see."

"It isn't Christmas yet."

"What's a few days, give or take? You spread enough cheer back there. The kids will never forget it."

Tears formed in her eyes, both at the extreme emotion she'd felt while doing her job and at Bo's acknowledgment of it.

"It meant a lot to me too," she said quietly.

He reached across the space and took her hand. She let him, loving the strong feel of his fingers wrapping around hers. Now would be an excellent time to tell him how she felt, but something kept her silent.

She'd call it cold feet but he'd call it stubbornness. She could see his point now, that she often bucked the system just because she'd been born to it in the Knight family. She'd spent a lifetime trying to prove herself to her brothers, to be one of the guys while still playing dolls and dress-up with her much more girly twin.

She had always been caught in between two worlds, but lately she'd come to realize she could be both the hardcore Marine Tyler as well as the woman who enjoyed slipping into a scrap of lace and luring in her man.

My man.

She stared at Bo's profile, rugged and so handsome that just looking at him made her insides warm. The man was everything a woman could want—a muscled badass with all the swagger to make a woman weak in the knees. He was also attuned to his feminine side, which meant he was good at understanding her. And damn fun to shop with too.

After a few minutes of comfortable silence, Bo guided the Humvee into a parking lot. The hotel rose up in the low skyline, with gray-blue stone that set it apart from the other buildings. The glass windows were darkened and made everything look sleek and expensive.

Mouth dropping open, she looked to Bo. "We're staying here?"

He threw her a grin. "Yes, and don't even think about requesting separate rooms."

Her jaw dropped farther. She hadn't been thinking anything along those lines, but then again, he didn't know that she'd had all day to think about what he'd said to her.

By the time they went inside, she was humming with nerves. She'd never told somebody she loved him before, because well, she never had. But with Hawk, the two halves of herself were able to come out and no one could appreciate them like he did.

After he paid for the room, he waved a hand for her to enter the elevator. The gray, glossy walls gave a blurry reflection of them standing stiffly side by side.

Tyler dragged in a deep breath, her nose filling with Bo's masculine musk.

Suddenly, she turned to him. Her heart gave one hard thud — and then she climbed him like a tree. Wrapping her arms around his neck and claiming his lips for her own even as she locked her thighs around his strong hips. He groaned and she thrust her tongue into his mouth, tasting a hint of sweetness like he'd stolen some candy from one of the kids.

He whipped around and pinned her to the wall of the elevator. The wild need in her fed into their kiss and ignited him too. He grabbed at her ass, pulling her up and into his growing erection.

"How many more floors?"

He didn't break the kiss. "Too many." He tongue-fucked her again until she was trembling for more.

By the time the doors opened, she was burning. He stumbled out and let her slide down his body. She felt every hard inch, landing on her boots lightly.

"This way." He caught her by the hand and pulled her down the corridor. When they reached the room, he had them inside and the door deadbolted behind them in a second.

"Get your clothes off," he ordered, eyes dark with desire.

Her own lust must be mirrored in her gaze. She raised her chin toward him. "You first."

"Fine." He whipped his shirt up and off, throwing it aside and advancing on her a step.

She backed up and tore off her top, tossing it away too.

They stared at each other, and she realized they were equally matched in all ways.

By some unspoken agreement, they went for the fly of their pants at the same time and in seconds had boots and clothes in a heap on the floor. Locked in an embrace, they fell to the bed, flesh to flesh.

Lips to lips.

He hovered over her, gazing deep into her eyes.

"Bo."

"You wish to tell me something?" Damn the man for expecting to hear the words she'd been withholding, but he deserved that much. The hard tip of his arousal brushed against her wet folds, making her ache to feel him stretching her. But he didn't seem in a hurry to move.

"Damn you for being so patient." She pushed upward, and his cock slipped across her straining clit.

A crooked smile formed at the corner of his mouth. "Some would call it a virtue."

She drew in a deep breath. He wasn't going to sate her need if she didn't tell him how she felt, and she had no reason to hold back any longer.

Cupping his angular jaw, she met his gaze. "Bo, I'm..."

He waited, zeroing in on her.

"I'm in love with you."

He fell still and only his Adam's apple bobbed as he swallowed. All of a sudden, he closed his eyes and dropped his forehead to hers. "Fuck, I never knew it would feel so good to hear those words."

She brushed her lips across his. "I love you."

He moaned, and she kissed him harder.

"I love you."

He opened his eyes. "Say it one more time."

"Only if your cock's inside me, because I can't wait anymore."

With a half-laugh, half-grunt, he joined them. Gliding balls-deep in one smooth stroke. She threw her head back on a moan of ecstasy. "I love you, Bo. Now move."

His laugh vibrated her as he began to churn his hips. Rooting his cock deep and then withdrawing with maddening slowness. Her wet walls gripped at him, urging him back inside and his hard body pressed against her clit with each movement.

She spread her legs wider, giving him full depth. He grunted as he felt the change and doubled his efforts, fucking her faster and faster.

There was no going slow, and they had no reason to hold back anymore. They were in love, and together they'd figure out the rest of their lives. Clinging to his shoulders, she met his every thrust and swished her tongue over his until the need grew unbearable. Her insides tightened, and she began to pulsate, milking his cock.

The long, low groan that left his throat rumbled through her, and his first spurt had her crying out. They peaked together, giving and taking, locked in the cloud of love surrounding them.

When she came to her senses, Bo lay on his side, his gaze warm and filled with love. She felt it like a caress to her bare skin, her heart, her soul.

"I'd say the day was a success, Knight."

She buried her face against his shoulder. "While I was doing all that work passing out gifts, where were you?"

His lips tightened.

Leaning on an elbow, she forced him to meet her stare. "What happened, Bo?"

"There was a small matter to attend to. We took care of it."

"Okayyy," she slowly drawled.

"You know it's classified."

"Yes, but you know you can talk to me about anything, right? If you need to unload...—"

He brushed his knuckles across her cheekbone, searching her eyes. "I will," he cut her off.

She tipped her head into his touch. "Good. Now there's the matter of my family to discuss."

A smile ghosted over his lips. "They're probably going to waterboard me when we get Stateside tomorrow."

She smacked at him even though she wouldn't put it past that rough Knight crew. "We'll have Lexi on our side."

"Right."

"You know there are still about thirty children who couldn't list a next of kin, right?"

His brows crinkled. "Yes, I heard. What's going to happen?"

"Well, I was thinking..."

He narrowed his eyes. "Go on."

"That we might stay here, just make sure those kids that aren't reunited right away are cared for and aren't as afraid. Plus, wouldn't it be nice for us to celebrate the holiday in a more meaningful way this year?"

He blinked a few times, and when she looked closer, she saw his eyes were shiny with tears. "How did I ever get such an amazing woman?" he asked thickly.

She cuddled closer and he pulled her atop him. When she straddled him, she found he was hard all over again. Pressing her lips to his, she sank down over his length. "We both got lucky."

Epilogue

As they pulled up to the Knights' home, the twinkle lights offered a glowing welcome and one that brought nervous jitters to Tyler's stomach. For the first time, she'd enter with Bo — as a couple.

He cut the engine and placed a hand over her knotted fingers in her lap. She pivoted her head to look at him. Her breath hitched as she stared at him — her man.

An amused smile graced his hard lips. "I can read your thoughts clearly on your face, baby. You'd better get control of that before we walk through that door, unless you want your family knowing you want to jump all this." He ran his hand down his chest, over the button-up shirt and a jacket that was broad enough to span even his broad shoulders.

She couldn't help but glance down at his jeans and sure enough, a bulge was evident. "Well, if my face gives away how much I want you, then that gives you away." She twitched her head toward his lap.

He chuckled. "Guilty. I can't wait to peel those skinny jeans off you, baby."

She looked down at herself. After returning to the States, they'd holed up in his apartment to sleep off the jetlag and then he'd insisted they must go get a big breakfast and go shopping for something she could wear to dinner with her family.

She had to admit the fitted black top, dark denim and heels and gold bangle bracelets made her feel as strong and confident as her military camo, and she'd take any help she could get to face her family right now.

Drawing a deep breath, she caught the notes of Bo's aftershave and nearly groaned. What she wouldn't do to kiss him all over, starting at the top and making her way down to the bottom, hitting the highlights along the way.

He snapped his fingers in front of her face. "Tyler."

"Yes, I'm ready." She opened the door of his jeep and climbed out. Careful how she stepped in her heels on the gravel drive, she made her way to the front door. A wreath hung there with what could only be Lexi's touch—a banner attached to the wreath that said Welcome to the Knights.

Bo's hand on her lower back kept her from shaking too much as she reached for the door handle. "Here we go," she said.

He laughed. "We aren't storming a bunker full of terrorists. Buck up, woman. We're only facing down your *maman* and *papa*, five brothers and sister."

201

"You're such a charming man. No wonder I love you." Sarcasm dripped from her voice as she pushed open the door to the sound of laughter and clanking noises coming from the kitchen.

Gripping Bo's hand, she entered the living room. There sat her *papa* in his recliner, watching two of her brothers play a dance video game. Her jaw dropped on a grin when Sean and Dylan made some hip moves.

"Ohhhh, dude! I won that round! Did you see my score?" Dylan elbowed Sean.

All the ladies who were gathered there cracked up laughing, and Tyler raised her voice to say, "Nice dancin', guys. Didn't know you had those kind of moves."

Everyone whipped around to look at her.

Then Bo.

Then their joined hands.

She watched her father's face, and when he showed no sign of fury, she looked to her brothers. She'd known her father would have no problem with anybody she chose as long as the man was good and she was happy. But her brothers, being friends with Bo, were another situation entirely.

Sean's stare shot to Bo's and there was a long heartbeat of silence as the two men sized each other up.

Irritation rose up in her. "Oh for God's sake. He's your buddy and what problem could you possibly have with him being with me?" She planted her free hand on her hip.

Dylan's wife Athena glided off the sofa in her graceful way and came forward to embrace Tyler. "You look radiant, dear. We're so glad you're home safe."

Sean's wife continued to stare, which made Tyler fidget. If anyone would shoot down her and Bo's relationship it would be Elise, the woman who called herself his best friend and ex-wife.

As the woman stood, Tyler edged a little closer to Bo, and he curved a hand around her waist, holding her in place.

Elise stepped up in front of them and shook her head. "I didn't believe it when Sean told me the rumor, but now that I see you two together, I don't know how I missed it before. You two were made for each other."

Tyler waited for more from her sister-in-law. When Elise lunged forward, arms flung wide to embrace them both, Tyler wrapped an arm around her back, overflowing with affection and relief.

When they drew apart, Tyler looked to Sean as Bo and Elise embraced.

Her brother still wore a skeptical crease between his brows. She opened her mouth to speak, but Bo flicked his head toward the door. "Gather your brothers and meet me outside. Let's settle this."

Sucking in a harsh gasp, Tyler reached for Bo. "No! You guys can't do this."

Her father stood from his recliner and came to stand between his sons and Bo. "Sean, Dylan, this is unnecessary. Tyler's a grown woman and able to make her own choices, same as you."

Her heart squeezed with love for her father.

"Ben, Chaz, Roades," Sean called. "Outside."

Releasing Bo's hand, she got in her brother's face. "Stop being a jerk, Sean. What do you care if I love Bo?"

At Sean's call, not only her brothers filled the room but her mother and the rest of her sisters-in-law too. Lexi trailed in last and when she saw what was happening, she plastered a hand over her mouth, eyes worried above.

Bo turned for the door.

Panic set in. Her lover was a badass, but he couldn't handle five Knights at once. Dammit, she'd left her weapon at Bo's place or she'd pop a shot off into a tree just to put a stop to her brothers' antics.

Bo stepped outside and her brothers filed out behind him, faces grim.

Tyler watched them for a moment, frozen to the floorboards. All of a sudden, reality hit and she ran outside with everyone else on her heels.

Bo stood in the middle of the yard, arms outstretched to make himself a big target. "Here I am, boys. Do your worst, but it won't change the way I feel about your sister."

"You should have fucking told us," Sean bit off.

"It's between me and Tyler, not you. You gonna throw a punch or what?" Bo egged him on.

"No!" Tyler launched into the yard to stand in front of the man she loved, prepared to stop the posse of angry Knights who obviously wanted a piece of him. "You leave him alone. I'm the one who started this."

Two of her brothers exchanged a look. "That doesn't make us feel any better, Tyler," Chaz drawled.

"Well, it's true—accept it or don't."

"Tyler, step aside." Ben's tone was deadly calm, sending chills all over her arms and up the back of her neck.

"Boys, this is ridiculous. We should all be giving Tyler and Bo our blessings," *Maman* spoke up.

The sisters-in-law said nothing, which made Tyler realize something must be up. That this was planned out and they knew the details.

Casting a look from face to face, Tyler finally settled on the one of the group who wasn't as poker-faced as the rest. Ben's wife Dahlia dropped her stare down and to the right.

A big plastic tub sat next to the front door.

Tyler started forward to get a good look at what was in the tub, when one of her brothers yelled, "Fire!"

She was trampled by a thousand pounds of muscle as they stormed their way to the tub. Something flew by her ear, followed by several more somethings. She straightened up in time to see the round objects striking Bo and breaking, leaving wet splotches all over his clothes.

Her mind cleared. Water balloons.

Gasps and laughter came from the women as Bo got drenched. But when some of the balloons just bounced off him and didn't break, he stooped to pick them up, gathered in one giant hand.

"Who wants it?" he threatened, looking at each of her brothers.

Tyler let out a peal of laughter. "Give 'em hell, babe!"

"Babe? Damn, she really is in love," Dylan muttered. She stalked to the tub and fished out a balloon of her own, rifling it straight at his head.

Five minutes later, all the balloons lay broken on the grass. Bo was drenched but several of her brothers had taken hits too.

She met Bo's gaze and love struck her so hard, she had no idea her feet were moving until she was in his arms. All six-feet-two of his hard, wet body molded around hers, and they kissed for all to see.

Hoots went up from Lexi and her *maman*, and then everyone began to applaud.

Grinning against Bo's lips, she said, "I think they've accepted us as a couple now."

He chuckled. "I think they're still gunning for me, and this might be a feud that goes on for years. But I've got some ammunition of my own for them."

They shared a smile and stepped away from each other, hands still clinging. "Everyone," Tyler said in a louder voice, "this is the man I'm going to spend my life with, Bo Hawkeye."

* * * * *

One of Tyler's brothers had found Bo some old sweats to put on since his clothes were soaked, and the rest of the dinner with Tyler's family was only good humor and cheer.

But when talk turned to the New Year, Bo felt himself sobering. He and Tyler had a lot of things to hammer out if they were making their relationship work. After all, she was due back at base and he'd be sent to God knew where as soon as a threat cropped up.

After dinner, Bo spent some time talking to her father, who asked about their intentions for the future, and it bothered Bo that he didn't have any answers. As soon as he got her back to his place, they were going to have a heart-to-heart.

People said that love could withstand the heavy storms that life threw at them, and he was very prepared to deal with anything to keep Tyler. But starting out with so much uncertainty hanging over them was making him nervous.

During the ride back to his place, she threw him some looks that said she'd picked up on his mood. When he got her inside his apartment and closed the door, she burst out, "Your silence is scary, Bo. What the hell's going on in your head?"

Amusement tipped the corner of his lips. "I'm surprised it took you that long to ask." He deadbolted the door and then turned to face her.

She cocked her hip, hand firmly planted there. "You'd better start talking. You've been quiet since you talked to my *papa*."

As always, he wasn't surprised at the keen observations she made. He took a step toward her, and she dodged him.

"You're not touching me until you tell me what my father said to you to make you upset."

He followed her, and she sidestepped, coming up against a table where he tossed down his keys. He closed his fingers around her upper arms and drew her against his chest. He felt a small shiver run through her.

Bowing his nose into her hair, he said, "It's not that bad, baby. I'm sorry for worrying you so much. Let's go to the bedroom and talk."

"Oh no. As soon as we cross that threshold, we'll be naked and kissin'."

He eyed her, burning with want within a blink.

"No," she said firmly, leading him to the sofa. She plopped down and waited for him to do the same. He drew her down to rest her head in his lap, mostly to disarm her. He knew all too well how much of a fight she put up and if they could get through this conversation without an argument, then he'd succeeded.

Her hair spread over his thighs, and his balls clenched, but he ignored his desires. Threading his fingers into her hair, he said, "We need to discuss the future."

She swallowed hard. "I know we do. I've been thinking a lot about it. I actually spoke with my commanding officer yesterday."

He started. "You did?"

"Yes, I wanted to straighten some ideas out in my head before I brought it up to you."

He stroked her hair. "Let me hear your thoughts."

She sat up and remained close but tucked her feet beneath her, facing him. "I asked to transfer someplace else, and my CO told me that wasn't possible. That I could remain doing what I do or I can take another position." She trailed off and took a deep breath.

"When did this even happen, baby? Why didn't you tell me?"

"You went out for a bit. Speaking of, where did you go?" She squeezed his hand.

He gave her a sly grin. "You'll find out soon enough."

"I know I will," she said with confidence and a smirk.

"So the old post isn't off the table. You can always return and we'll figure things out."

She gave him a soft smile, love in her eyes. "I thought we could weigh the decisions together."

He smiled. "All right. Tell me the options."

"First is you move to South Carolina with me and transfer to another division of Operation Freedom Flag."

He loved leading Team Rou and Louisiana was in his blood, but he'd make the switch if it meant being with the woman he loved.

"The other option is that I stay here and be part of OFFSUS."

He stilled, working out the angles of that revelation in a heartbeat. "You spoke with Jackson."

She nodded. "He called right after I finished speaking with my CO, and I took it as a sign. He said they were so impressed with me in Kandahar that they wanted me to stay around here, at the ready as civil affairs specialist."

Pride expanded his chest and he suddenly felt choked up. "God, baby, that's such a pat on the back coming from Jackson."

She smiled. "I know. I'm guessing they're rare handouts too."

"Damn straight. And my woman got one."

Her smile widened.

So," he said with caution, not wanting to sound too hopeful about her taking option B and staying in Louisiana, "have you made a decision?"

She chewed her lower lip and the skin plumped, making her lips entirely more kissable. He tore his gaze away and focused. But if she didn't respond soon he was going to toss her down and have his way with her.

"I've made a choice, and I hope you're ready for it."

He waited. She let the moment and tension swell out.

"That's it." He reached for her.

Letting out a burst of laughter, she said, "I decided to take Jackson's offer."

"Oh God." He yanked her across his lap, her round ass settled against his groin, and wrapped his arms around her tight. She was everything he could wish for no matter what she decided, but here she'd have connections of family and friends and they could build their life together. He kissed her hard. "As long as you're happy, baby, I am."

"It makes sense for me to remain near you and my family. Besides, it's a step up from training new recruits and after working with those kids in

211

Kandahar, I knew I wanted something that would do more good in the world."

He gave a slow shake of his head. "You're so amazing. It's a wonder I didn't see it sooner."

She lifted a shoulder in a shrug. "It happened when the time was right."

He ground his hips upward, pushing his erection into the V of her thighs. She went boneless in his hold, hanging forward with her lips a breath from his.

"I have a surprise for you," he said.

She made a noise in her throat. "Is this about where you went early this morning?"

"Mmm-hmm." He skimmed his hands up her spine, eager to get at all that silky skin beneath her top.

"Are you gonna make me drag it out of you?" She reached for the button of his jeans. When she popped it and dipped a finger in to find the swollen head of his cock right there, their breathing came faster.

Suddenly, he dumped her off his lap, leaving her hair hanging over one blazing eye, and stood. "Wait here." He moved to the coat closet where he'd hidden away a package. "Close your eyes."

He glanced to see if she was listening, and then he pulled out the big red-wrapped gift with a huge gold bow. Keeping it concealed behind his back in case she was peeking — he wouldn't put it past her — he walked back to the sofa and sat.

She sat before him, long, dark lashes sweeping across the tops of her cheekbones. Her cheeks were pink with excitement and she was chewing her lip again, which was driving him wild.

Placing the package in her hands, he said, "Open your eyes."

She didn't immediately, just ran her hands over the gift like a little kid on Christmas. She lifted it and shook it.

"I'm going to have a crazy life with you, Tyler."

Her eyes popped open, and she saw his grin. "I think we'll keep each other on our toes. Why did you go out and buy me a gift?"

"It bothered me that I didn't have anything to give you back in Kandahar. It was Christmas and I wanted to make up for it."

She let out a slow breath and then hooked a hand around his nape. "I love you, Bo."

"You're my world, baby."

Eyes gleaming with emotion, she ripped into the paper. Inside the rectangular box were layers of tissue paper and finally she drew out a whisper of red lace dangling from her index finger.

Her wide eyes said it all.

"Maybe we can find a closet where you can change," he said, voice rumbling low with all the desire inside him.

She hopped off the couch and twitched her hips all the way to the bedroom, the nightie trailing the floor as she went. "You've got one minute, Hawkeye. Then you'd better report for duty."

He didn't bother smothering the growl emerging past his lips. He started counting. When he walked into the bedroom to find her naked and just drawing the lace over her curvaceous body, his eyes hooded.

He approached her slowly and caught the quiver rolling over her. Grabbing her around the waist, he spun her off her feet and pressed her to the nearest wall. A gasp sounded, which he swallowed on a sweep of his tongue.

Small noises left her as he kissed and fondled her breasts through the red lace and then ran his hand down the flat of her stomach until he reached her soaking pussy. Her folds were slick and engorged in anticipation, and she swiveled her hips to get closer to his touch.

Passion doubled inside him as he stroked her into her first orgasm. When she was panting and clinging to him to stay upright, he stared down into her eyes. "Happy New Year, baby. I'm going to spend the entire holiday making you scream, so be prepared to explain to your family over black-eyed peas and collard greens why you're hoarse."

Tossing back her head, she laughed. "We might be late to New Year's dinner."

He latched onto her throat with his lips, and her laugh transformed to a moan. He lifted her, and she wrapped her toned thighs around him. They hit the bed.

She pulled him down to kiss him deeply. When she drew back, her eyes glimmered with love and mischief. "Let the celebration begin."

READ ON FOR A SNEAK PEEK OF ANGEL OF THE KNIGHT, BOOK 7 OF THE KNIGHT OPS SERIES

"Catch ya later, assholes," Matthew Rock called out to the guys of Knight Ops and received two waves, a salute and a middle finger in return.

Laughing as he climbed behind the wheel of his SUV, his back muscle gave a sharp twinge.

Too many hours frozen in the same position, rifle resting on his knee and the sights aimed on the dumb fucker who was trafficking humans. The guy had evaded Homeland Security for more than a year and sent hundreds of women, young men and children into service in the United States as house slaves, sex slaves and worse.

But this time Knight Ops had finally been called in to deal with him, and their special ops unit never failed.

He rolled down the window to drink in some of the cooler breeze coming off the Gulf and backed out of the parking spot on the military base.

"Not if I catch you first, Rocko," his team captain Ben called back.

Rocko threw a wave, and from the corner of his eye, caught a scrap of red on the passenger's seat.

He slammed on the brakes. Lace and silk.

Fuck.

Only one woman would put those panties in his vehicle.

Only one even existed in Rocko's world.

Since realizing his feelings ran deeper for her than anything a one-night stand could provide, he hadn't had a woman in too many months to count. When he'd begun working with the five Knight brothers, he'd never guessed he'd take one look at their baby sister and know she was the woman he wanted for the rest of his life.

Lexi Knight.

L'il sis was guarded like fucking royalty, and every time she got a boyfriend, the guys would hunt him down and warn him off. Of course, Lexi's taste in men sucked—she seemed to gravitate to the worst of the male sex.

But it was also the primary reason Rocko had spent years battling his own desires and shooting down every advance the woman threw his way.

This time, panties.

Red. Silk. Panties.

He tentatively reached across the console and closed his fingers on the smooth fabric, imagining her warmth still clung to the fibers as he drove out of the parking lot and away from any of her brothers who might see him bring the panties to his nose.

He inhaled deeply.

Jesus Christ. They were worn.

The sweet, musky scent of pussy filled his nose and had his cock standing straight up against the fly of his cargo pants.

He lowered the garment, eyes blurred with fantasies of nudging her golden tan thighs apart and opening his mouth over her wet pussy.

God, it was like a drug gift-wrapped in one lace-edged scrap of cloth. Pure torment.

With them gripped in his fist, he brought them back to his nose and inhaled.

The faint trace of Lexi's perfume filled his head. A sort of citrus with underlying notes of flowers.

The woman was going to drive him off the deep end.

His cock head swelled and he felt precum seeping from the tip to wet his briefs.

He had two choices — drive over to the Knights and reach under Lexi's skirt to see if she was bare-assed. Or drive home and ignore her overture to get him into her bed.

What was the worst her brothers could do to him? Kill him and bury him came to mind, but surely they were too good of friends to off one of their team members.

Maiming was another story.

Rocko brought the panties back to his nose. Fuck, she was sweeter than he'd fantasized. How the hell could he ever look at her the same way again?

That was what she was counting on—that he'd scale that wall between her and her brothers like he was storming a fucking fortress. Hell, he couldn't deny he wanted that. One glance down at the bulge in his pants could attest to how much pent-up need he harbored in his very blue balls.

She's off-limits.

Not only because of her overprotective family but Rocko had always known that he was no good for Lexi. He'd never be there enough. She needed—deserved—a man who worked nine-to-five and came home to kiss his wife before dinner and then take her to bed and show her just how much he appreciated her.

What could Rocko offer her besides a lifetime of fearing he would never return home? That if he did, the mission might wear on him. Render him silent.

Sure, he handled stress better than many Marines he'd seen, but he hid a hell of a lot behind his easy smiles too. He stuffed it down, same as when his mother had left him and his sister to be raised by their father.

He was a good dad, did the best he could. But he wasn't around a lot since he worked to support them and that left Rocko in charge.

Now his father was dead and Rocko couldn't even talk to him about any of this.

He opened his fist over the passenger's seat to release Lexi's gift. But before he dropped them, he brought them back to his nose. God, what a fucking pervert he was, but she'd counted on him being enough of one to taunt him into making a move.

As he inhaled deeply, his phone rang.

He dropped the panties into his lap, trying not to think of Lexi's round ass seated there, molded against his steely erection, and answered the cell.

"Rocko."

Ben's voice filled his ear. "Lexi just called. She's got some party for us tonight."

He closed his eyes momentarily. He couldn't trust himself to get within a Louisiana mile of the woman right now, not with her tight curves and sweet pussy on his mind.

"Can't make it," he grated out.

"Bullshit. What do you have planned besides going home and beating off?"

He didn't have any idea how close to the truth that was.

Swallowing, Rocko glanced down at the red panties in his lap. "I can't make it," he said again.

"Lexi won't take no for an answer."

Of course she wouldn't. The woman was relentless—and going to get him beaten to a pulp by her brothers for giving in to her.

If he was smart, he'd toss her panties out the window and drive to his lonely, dull, beige apartment instead of going to the Knights' big, cozy house filled with flowers Lexi brought home to be tormented by the most beautiful, desirable woman in the universe.

Ben went on, "It's some kind of strawberry festival. Now, don't break my little sister's heart. She's far too sweet for the likes of you and the least you can do is show up and eat some shortcake." Ben's words hit like grenades.

She *was* too sweet for the likes of him.

How many times had he considered giving in and taking her? Only knowing he couldn't finish the job and end the fling with her standing before a minister and wearing white had stopped him.

"I already got an invitation," he said huskily. Strawberry-colored panties from the woman herself.

"Good, then see ya there."

Rocko ended the call and fingered the garment in his lap again. Dammit, he didn't have much choice but to go. What then? He couldn't exactly walk in and look at Lexi, knowing she'd given him the panties right off her body. That if he threw her skirt up and bent her over, he could sink balls-deep into her tight pussy.

He let out a heavy sigh and turned the vehicle toward the Knights' place.

Fuck, he was in so much trouble. After battling Lexi's bold advances for the entire past year, Rocko's control was slipping fast and furious.

This time he didn't know if he could stop himself from laying claim to the Knights' sister.

1-CLICK YOUR COPY OF ANGEL OF THE KNIGHT ON   AMAZON!

Em Petrova

Em Petrova was raised by hippies in the wilds of Pennsylvania but told her parents at the age of four she wanted to be a gypsy when she grew up. She has a soft spot for babies, puppies and 90s Grunge music and believes in Bigfoot and aliens. She started writing at the age of twelve and prides herself on making her characters larger than life and her sex scenes hotter than hot.

She burst into the world of publishing in 2010 after having five beautiful bambinos and figuring they were old enough to get their own snacks while she pounds away at the keys. In her not-so-spare time, she is fur-mommy to a Labradoodle named Daisy Hasselhoff and works as editor with USA Today and New York Times bestselling authors.

Find Em Petrova at empetrova.com

Other Indie Titles by Em Petrova

West Protection
HIGH-STAKES COWBOY
RESCUED BY THE COWBOY
GUARDED BY THE COWBOY
COWBOY CONSPIRACY THEORY
COWBOY IN THE CORSSHAIRS

PROTECTED BY THE COWBOY

Xtreme Ops
HITTING XTREMES
TO THE XTREME
XTREME BEHAVIOR
XTREME AFFAIRS
XTREME MEASURES
XTREME PRESSURE
XTREME LIMITS
Xtreme Ops Alaska Search and Rescue
NORTH OF LOVE

Crossroads
BAD IN BOOTS
CONFIDENT IN CHAPS
COCKY IN A COWBOY HAT
SAVAGE IN A STETSON
SHOW-OFF IN SPURS

Dark Falcons MC
DIXON
TANK
PATRIOT
DIESEL

BLADE

The Guard
HIS TO SHELTER
HIS TO DEFEND
HIS TO PROTECT

Moon Ranch
TOUGH AND TAMED
SCREWED AND SATISFIED
CHISELED AND CLAIMED

Ranger Ops
AT CLOSE RANGE
WITHIN RANGE
POINT BLANK RANGE
RANGE OF MOTION
TARGET IN RANGE
OUT OF RANGE

Knight Ops Series
ALL KNIGHTER
HEAT OF THE KNIGHT
HOT LOUISIANA KNIGHT
AFTER MIDKNIGHT
KNIGHT SHIFT

ANGEL OF THE KNIGHT
O CHRISTMAS KNIGHT

Wild West Series
SOMETHING ABOUT A LAWMAN
SOMETHING ABOUT A SHERIFF
SOMETHING ABOUT A BOUNTY HUNTER
SOMETHING ABOUT A MOUNTAIN MAN

Operation Cowboy Series
KICKIN' UP DUST
SPURS AND SURRENDER

The Boot Knockers Ranch Series
PUSHIN' BUTTONS
BODY LANGUAGE
REINING MEN
ROPIN' HEARTS
ROPE BURN
COWBOY NOT INCLUDED
COWBOY BY CANDLELIGHT
THE BOOT KNOCKER'S BABY
ROPIN' A ROMEO
WINNING WYOMING

Ménage à Trouble Series

WRANGLED UP
UP FOR GRABS
HOOKING UP
ALL WOUND UP
DOUBLED UP novella duet
UP CLOSE
WARMED UP

Another Shot at Love Series
GRIFFIN
BRANT
AXEL

Rope 'n Ride Series
BUCK
RYDER
RIDGE
WEST
LANE
WYNONNA

The Dalton Boys
COWBOY CRAZY Hank's story
COWBOY BARGAIN Cash's story
COWBOY CRUSHIN' Witt's story
COWBOY SECRET Beck's story

COWBOY RUSH Kade's Story
COWBOY MISTLETOE a Christmas novella
COWBOY FLIRTATION Ford's story
COWBOY TEMPTATION Easton's story
COWBOY SURPRISE Justus's story
COWGIRL DREAMER Gracie's story
COWGIRL MIRACLE Jessamine's story
COWGIRL HEART Kezziah's story

Single Titles and Boxes
THE BOOT KNOCKERS RANCH BOX SET
THE DALTON BOYS BOX SET
SINFUL HEARTS
JINGLE BOOTS
A COWBOY FOR CHRISTMAS
FULL RIDE

Club Ties Series
LOVE TIES
HEART TIES
MARKED AS HIS
SOUL TIES
ACE'S WILD

Firehouse 5 Series
ONE FIERY NIGHT

CONTROLLED BURN
SMOLDERING HEARTS

Hardworking Heroes Novellas
STRANDED AND STRADDLED
DALLAS NIGHTS
SLICK RIDER
SPURRED ON

EM PETROVA
WWW.EMPETROVA.COM

Made in the USA
Monee, IL
06 October 2023

44092251R00129